TROUBLE AFOOT

BENJAMIN BRADLEY

INDIES UNITED PUBLISHING HOUSE, LLC
P.O. BOX 3071
QUINCY, IL 62305-3071

First Edition published September 2021

Published by Indies United Publishing House, LLC

ISBN: 978-1-64456-365-6

Library of Congress Control Number: 2021943634

INDIES UNITED PUBLISHING HOUSE, LLC
P.O. BOX 3071
QUINCY, IL 62305-3071

For J.R.

"Everyone is a moon, and has a dark side which he never shows to anybody."
  Samuel Langhorne Clemens

CHAPTER ONE

THE BEAST LOOKED BIGGER than anything Taylor had ever seen before. Taller than anything that belonged in a forest, aside from Narnia or maybe something from the Lord of the Rings. The creature's eyes looked fake, rubbery, but somehow emotive in the distant fog from the morning dew.

Taylor blinked his eyes, rubbed at them, and squinted again. Waited for the image to clear. To refresh. But the beast remained. Staring at him. Cold, lifeless eyes. Like something out of a comic book or a horror movie. Every muscle in Taylor's body tightened. He whispered, but no words came out. Just an exhale that bordered on a quiet groan. Fear sounded different than anything else.

Moving in slow motion, he tapped Cooper's leg. Cooper let out a half-snore, groaned, and murmured to himself as he adjusted his position in the beach chair. "Ten more minutes…"

Out of the corner of his mouth, Taylor whispered. This time, words emerged. "Open your eyes, Coop."

Taylor couldn't take his eyes off of it. It stood far away, somewhere near fifty yards from their shoreline fishing spot. Unlike

1

anything he'd ever seen before. He kicked Cooper again. Harder this time. Cooper let out a yelp. The creature didn't move. Just stared. Like he was trying to communicate. To signal something. Taylor's throat went dry. The pounding in his chest sounded like the beat of a kick drum. Everything inside of him braced for the worst.

"Look over there..." Taylor whispered.

Cooper grabbed his fishing pole and pulled. "Nothing still?"

"Look over there..." Taylor whispered again.

"You know I can't hear you when you talk like that. What is going on with your face? You look like you've seen a ghost."

The beast moved. A step to the right. The leaves crunched into the ground beneath its feet. The early morning sun crept over the horizon and the shadows of the trees and brush flickered. Cooper caught on. He followed Taylor's gaze.

"Do you see it? Or am I losing my mind?" Taylor whispered.

"Not sure those two are mutually exclusive, but I see it."

"Is it.... What is it?"

"Maybe a bear. Maybe a hunter in camo."

"Are there bears in North Carolina?"

"I mean, not around here, but maybe it got lost. Escaped from the zoo or something."

"Have you ever seen a bear before?"

"Yeah, on a boy scout trip as a kid in the Smokies."

"And did it look... did it look like this?"

Cooper shook his head. "No, but there are lots of kinds of bears and—"

The beast sprinted off. A crash in the leaves echoed and then faded into the distance. It moved on two feet. Like a human. It moved with familiarity, a comfort in the forest. Graceful and nimble.

"Well, that was weird." Cooper turned back and tugged at his rod. Taylor couldn't take his eyes off of the tree line. The forest was still. Typical for an early morning where fishermen

2

outnumber hikers. Ripples dissolved into the algae-lined water, which now sat tranquil as it held Cooper's bobber on the surface. Soil pushed out into ridges around the butt cap of Taylor's borrowed rod. The reel seat sat against the ground, resting atop pebbles and straw pine that would provide little resistance to the chomp of a curious creature underwater. Any momentary interest in the lake had disappeared the instant the beast moved into his eye line.

"Coop?" Taylor asked. His voice cracked under the pressure of the moment.

"Yes, Taylor? Are you going through puberty again or…"

"Did we just see… did we just see Bigfoot?"

Cooper let out a belly laugh and slapped his knee. "Because Bigfoot lives in suburban North Carolina. Good one. You get any sleep last night?"

"You didn't answer the question."

"Because it's not an actual question, right?"

"We need to tell somebody." Taylor stood, seized the moment of courage and pushed Cooper to move. "Get your stuff. Enough of this waiting around."

Cooper met his eyes and, after a moment of hesitation, nodded and pulled his line out of the murky water. They tiptoed towards where the beast once stood, every step unleashing a cacophony of crunches through the quiet morning. Taylor scoured the ground for a set of tracks. Nothing. No footprints. Not a trace. Cooper stood and watched with his arms crossed and a smile on his face.

After another ten minutes of searching, Taylor gave up. He waited for Cooper to dig into him for the fruitless search, for the unwarranted fear that he'd let overtake him. But nothing came. They began their trek out of the woods in silence. With each step, Taylor eyed the surrounding woods. Each thrash of a squirrel jumping into the leaves sounded like the crash of a cymbal. Sweat beaded on his brow. Each step he took was careful. Measured. Calculated.

3

Before long, they were at the car. Whether from tiredness or a newfound belief, Cooper had lowered his defenses and agreed to tag along as Taylor told the park rangers what he saw. Taylor stood with eyes on the forest behind them as Cooper tossed their cooler and chairs into the trunk of his car. Each dancing shadow looked suspicious. Every movement was alarming. Nothing was the same as before he'd seen that beast. Nothing.

CHAPTER TWO

THE LEAVES of the towering sourwood trees were bonfire red and stood in stark contrast to the sun-flame golds of the neighboring magnolias. Autumn had brought on cooler temperatures and stiff winds, but the sun hung in the sky like summer hadn't disappeared just yet. The hum of low-volume local news filled the tiny cab of Zoe Watt's truck as she steered away from her cottage and toward the front gate of Umstead State Park. Her tires sank into the soft soil next to the driveway, falling into well-worn grooves. She threw the gearshift into park and hopped out.

Six patient drivers waited at the gate, blasting heat through their vents to fight off the morning chill. Along the shoulder just outside the entrance, five other cars sat idle and cold as the dewdrops. Although four "NO PARKING" signs lined the soil, five gate-hoppers was a relatively meager crew. In Zoe's rookie days as a Park Ranger, she had marched along the street and written a ticket to each illegally parked vehicle. Nothing changed. If anything, more cars were parking there now than before.

The old beat-up teal Prius waiting at the front of the line was as familiar as the morning birdsong. Zoe beamed as she undid the combination lock, opened the gate and waved the traffic through. The Prius's driver stopped midway and waved. "Another beautiful day in Umstead!" The gray-haired woman shouted with more pluck than anybody should have at such an ungodly hour.

Zoe rolled her eyes. "I hope to be on your level of enthusiasm by my next cup of coffee, Donna Sue."

"If it takes two cups, you're drinking the wrong stuff." Donna Sue grinned and nodded. "More jerks parking on the shoulder, I see."

Zoe glanced toward the cars. Most were Subarus or hybrids, and most had a bike rack or straps.

"I know they mean no harm but darn, have some respect!" Donna Sue said.

"In their defense, our staff have their hands full elsewhere. Parking tickets have fallen on our priority list."

"And yet, here you are, glaring at them while you open the gate."

Zoe chuckled. "Who was that guy who rolled a rock up a hill for his entire life?"

"Sisyphus, I believe."

"That's the one. I'm thinking about changing my name to Sisyphus."

Donna Sue laughed with a vigor Zoe admired. Zoe tapped the roof of the car and waved her on. "Enjoy your run, ma'am."

Zoe cruised down the path after the bottleneck had cleared and switched the radio to music. Her presets were all classic rock and news stations, but she only used them when somebody else was in the truck. She'd grown to love the awful country radio stations despite broadcasting to the world that it was the music of back-country hillbillies and Hollywood love stories. North Carolina had that effect on people. It wore a person down. Without notice, Zoe was singing along to fast-paced banjo-induced rants about trucks and cold beer. She hadn't even admitted it to Gil. There was no guidebook on what little secrets of your world you should let your soon-to-be husband in on. She found cover under their shared love for all things CCR. She switched over to the CD player and the unmistakable opening chords of Bad Moon Rising rung out.

A squat Ford Ranger with the North Carolina State Parks logo on the side and a dented back tailgate approached from the south. A trash-picker and three split logs rattled around the truck bed as it neared. Zoe slowed to a crawl and faded the volume of John Fogerty's voice to a whisper. The smiling face of Clement Jenkins, accompanied by his thick-as-molasses southern accent, greeted her as she stopped.

"Thought you were opening today, mighty fine one we've got," he said.

"Not half bad. It'll warm up." Zoe looked to the cloudless blue sky. "I was just headed in to see Mathias. What's on your plate today?"

"Pulled the maintenance crew to help clear some brush off Sal's Branch Trail." Clem pulled a toothpick from his lips and picked between his teeth. "Storm the other night must've washed some gunk into the culvert. Looks like a dam, so I hear. We'll be busier than a one-legged cat in a sandbox!"

Zoe chuckled at the image. Clem's repertoire of southern sayings that meant absolutely nothing went on longer than a country mile. "Need a hand? I'd love to pitch in."

Clem grinned. "Mathias has you penciled in for desk duty. Joanne is still out."

Zoe's heart sank. "Shit, still? I thought I was free to roam this week."

"Think again, wild spirit." Clem returned the toothpick to his lips and smiled. "I'm off. Enjoy the shackles and recycled air of the Visitor's Center. Don't get a paper cut!"

Before Zoe could groan again, Clem had sped off. She considered doing a lap of the parking lots or picking up trash to kill time before the doldrums of the desk. Her instincts won out, and she went inside. Mathias could already see her truck from his office if he'd glanced out either of the two large, grime and pollen-caked windows. She swallowed her pride and steered toward the back, where a lone truck sat in the lot.

Each ranger had their own domain. Clem managed the foot trails used by hikers and runners. Ernest Henley, who was about as friendly as poison ivy, took care of the bridle trails, which were more often used by mountain bikers than horses in recent years. Mathias Wittles, the firm but fair leader of the pack who held the title of Park Superintendent, managed the budget, staffing, and all else that fell in-between. Zoe had drawn the short straw as the least-senior staff member and was in charge of volunteers. Despite many protests about how her degree in Environmental Science and Ecology didn't equip her to supervise troops of Boy Scouts and churchgoers, nothing had changed.

Zoe eyed the front desk with a loathing she reserved for assholes that littered or anybody who would dare speak ill of her beloved Creedence Clearwater Revival. She'd tried to talk her way out of the rotational position more times than she could count, but Mathias wouldn't hear it. His dispassionate response echoed around her brain as she slumped into the rickety wooden chair.

"Everybody takes a few hours here or there when we need it." Mathias tugged at his unruly mustache. "Until we can afford another full-time office worker on days Joanne has off, this is a team effort."

Raucous laughter sounded from the back office and out stumbled Ernest. The gray-beard of the ranger staff stepped out for patrol, laughing on his phone as he approached his truck. Zoe waited for her skin to match the pine needles as she turned green with envy as Ernest darted off towards the horse trails and sighed.

By nine, Zoe had handled two "emergency" phone calls from lost hikers and redirected them back to safety. She worked her way through a Sudoku without a mistake, then started a crossword.

Just as she parsed out the letters for ten across, the front doors opened and two out-of-breath teenagers tumbled in.

Zoe stood. "Can I help you boys?"

"We—" the taller one bent over like a sprinter after a race. He kept trying to talk, but almost hyperventilated.

"Take it easy, no rush here. Catch your breath," Zoe said. "Is somebody hurt?"

They both shook their heads. Relief washed over Zoe. Few things were worse than the panic that ensued after an injured hiker. Even if it was poor luck or the hiker's fault, the mountain of paperwork rivaled Everest. Plus, the whole park shut down. Trails grew crowded with rubberneckers. If there was such a thing as too many first responders showing up, it too often followed a sprained ankle on the trail.

"What are your names?"

The shorter one with a buzz cut introduced himself as Cooper. The taller one with a messy brown mop was Taylor. Cooper nudged his friend, who was still out of breath. "Go ahead, tell her."

"We saw something," Taylor took a deep breath, "In the woods."

Zoe reached into a file cabinet to her left and slapped the piece of paper onto the desktop. "Fill this out, please."

Taylor looked dumbfounded. "But, like, aren't you going to do something?"

"Is anybody in immediate danger?"

Taylor shook his head. "No, but somebody could be. We don't know where that beast went off to."

"I can complete this for you." Zoe slid the paper back her way. "Can you describe what you saw?"

"Well, it was earlier this morning. We'd set out to fish on the side trail off Big Lake around dawn." Taylor told the tale like it was a bedtime story. "We were just sitting there shooting the shit and all, and then we—"

"You," Cooper interrupted. "I saw nothing but a blur."

"Fine. *I* saw this, like, ape."

Zoe kept her eyes on the paper. "Okay, and how far away were you?"

"Hell, maybe half a football field?" Taylor looked to Cooper, who ignored him again. "It was down, like far away, but I know what I saw. It walked like a human."

Zoe tried to hide her grin. "And how big was this *ape?*"

"Tall." Taylor raised his hand above his own head. "Bigger than me, I'd guess."

"Mhm, and you?" Zoe turned to Cooper. "You were busy or didn't see it or…"

Cooper was stoic. "I fell asleep. This asshole wakes me up saying he saw Bigfoot and I—"

"I never said Bigfoot, Coop. I just—"

Zoe let their bickering simmer before finishing the paperwork. "Thank you both for your time." She pasted on her best marketing-material-park-ranger smile. "This is a helpful report. We'll put our best rangers on it."

The boys looked dumbfounded. "You're not scared?"

"Nope." Zoe leaned in to whisper. "I'll tell you a secret. We actually have a lot of wildlife in the park."

"Yeah, but… this was something else."

"From a distance, a lot of creatures can be hard to distinguish. I don't doubt that you saw something." Zoe tapped the completed report on the desk. "We'll send a truck out to look and if we see anything, we will clear the area to make sure nobody gets hurt."

Cooper snorted. "Told ya. Can we go now?"

Taylor sighed, and they exited together. Zoe watched them go and exhaled. Part of her was excited. Like a kid trying to sleep on Christmas Eve, knowing all too well that Santa was on his way. The other part of her was a realist. Kids will be kids. Plus, folks from the city tended to misjudge nature. There was little reason to give Taylor and Cooper's story more than a passing glance. Still, she followed procedure.

In perfect cursive, she dated the top of the report, stepped back into the bullpen of empty ranger desks and moved over to the corkboard in the center of the far wall. After successfully locating an orphan thumbtack, she pinned the report to the board, then added another pin on the park map next to the Big Lake side trail. A voice interrupted her train of thought.

"Another one?" Mathias asked, one hand on a coffee cup with the other on his hip.

He wiggled his nose and then swiped at a stray mustache hair that poked his nostril. Zoe turned to face him. "Another one."

CHAPTER THREE

COOL WINDS BLEW through the tops of the towering pines that decorated the inland stretches of Brewster, Massachusetts. The hustle and chaos of summer had come and passed, along with the flood of visitors that filled the restaurants, rentals, and beaches, all of which now stood empty. The deciduous trees mirrored the sandy shores as both had thinned out and left an empty presence behind.

"Keep your head down," Doris Marsh whispered.

Casper ducked down. He sat with his back against the cool stone exterior of the building, which felt like a block of ice. He turned the phone's camera back so it faced him.

"I don't know if we—"

Doris waved her hands. "Shush! I hired you, now deliver the goods."

Casper sighed and extended the phone over the lip of the window that looked into the sparse exercise room of the West Brewster Community Association Building. The cramped, four-room structure had seen few changes as it shifted from a single-family home into a shared space. The exorbitant costs ate into the

HOA's rainy day funds and then some, much to the ire of the residents, one of which was Doris Marsh.

"Higher, Casper. Come on now. I thought you were a professional."

Although her feet didn't move with the same grace as in her younger years, she could still find a person's soft spot and push like there was no tomorrow. Casper had learned that the hard way. He frowned. "I used to be. This isn't work for a private investigator, Doris."

Doris cleared her throat so loud it sounded like static on the line. "Says who? Am I mistaken that you tracked down both of Pearl Greene's ex-lovers?"

The mention of the word *lover* made him cringe. "No, but I—"

"And tell me again, what was the verdict?"

Casper sighed. "I really don't—"

"Answer your paying client's questions, Casper Kelly."

"Walter Daly has been divorced three times; each marriage shorter than the last. Pearl dodged a bullet."

"And the other one that got away?"

"Arthur Mulvaney was her high school boyfriend and since then he, uh—" Casper picked at blades of grass with his fingers and stared off into the distance.

"Ugly. He grew up ugly. Now you're telling me that a little snooping on my husband is above your pay grade?" Doris snorted. "I'll remember that when I'm cutting the check."

"Fine."

Casper shoved the phone upwards. Doris went quiet. For a second, Casper forgot he was a low-level detective for hire that the senior citizens of Brewster, Massachusetts, loved to call on for any minor task. There wasn't much crime, or much of anything, in the sleepy beachside hamlet of Brewster. Cape Cod, particularly in the off-season, was a ghost town. The big, mysterious case that brought him to the area was a one-hit-wonder. His caseload for the past three months was a mix of finding long-lost lovers of local senior citizens on Facebook and searching for a lost cat. Oh, and Doris.

"Casper?" Doris's tone was somber. "I've seen all I need to see." She pushed strands of her white hair around her ears.

He faced the screen again. "Is he there?"

She bit her lip and nodded. "And so was she."

Casper stood and brushed himself off. Blades of fresh-cut grass from the last mow of the season clung to his trousers. Small green stains scuffed the sides of his sneakers. "Think it's time we go talk with him?"

Doris looked at the ground. Casper decided for her, half to put an end to the case and half to put an end to her prolonged misery. He marched through the double-doors of the lobby, pushed through the hallway, and into the exercise room. His footsteps echoed in the cavernous space. Daniel Marsh stood in the center of the hardwood floor with one arm around the back of Fran Roach.

"How could you?" Doris shouted from the phone. Her voice cracked like a heartbroken teenager.

Casper held the screen closer to Daniel. Crow's feet had set in alongside deep wrinkles throughout his face. His thin, gray hair fell over his ears and the fluorescent overhead lights bounced off the baldness of his head. He squinted his eyes and looked at Casper. "Have we met?"

Casper pointed and Doris chimed in. "Down here, Daniel. It's me, Doe."

"Doe?" Daniel looked like somebody had just punched him in the gut. He squinted at the screen. "I can explain, I swear…"

Doris crossed her arms and looked away from the screen with a harrumph. "Go ahead."

Casper glanced at Fran, who had retreated to the back wall of the studio. He smiled at her and shrugged. She shook her head and laughed.

Daniel moved closer to the phone, still squinting. His voice shook, but he spoke just below a yell. "Honey, how well do you remember our first date?"

"September 16th, 1953. You took me to The Great Wazu for a hoagie because you couldn't afford a movie. We listened to the radio in your car and danced on the bluffs by the beach."

Daniel looked at Casper and smiled. "I was a romantic."

"What's your point?" Doris shouted.

"I... well, I know it's been a hard time, so I hired Fran here."

"Hired?" Doris grew animated. "What is she, some kind of call girl?"

Fran chuckled aloud, shook her head again and left the room. Casper mumbled. "Maybe I should just give the phone to—"

"You move an inch and you are toast, Casper Kelly." Doris's voice boomed. "Use your detective skills for once in your life. Tell me what's going on here."

Casper glanced at Daniel, who had twisted his face with a mix of confusion and regret. "Ma'am, I think your husband may be able to fill you in on that better than I."

"You mean my ex-husband?" Doris shouted. Daniel cringed at her tone. "The one who we just caught having a fling with a mid-forties floozy?"

Daniel turned bright red. He mumbled at first and then shouted so loud it echoed through the empty studio. "I was getting dance lessons!"

Doris stared at her phone. "What was that?"

"Dance lessons."

"Dance lessons?" Doris said.

Casper turned the phone back to himself. "Dance lessons."

Daniel continued. "Fran teaches ballroom dance at the Community College. I wanted to learn how to dance like we used to. My body just doesn't move..." Before he could go on, Casper tossed the phone to Daniel and jogged out of the room.

Ten minutes later, Daniel hobbled down the front steps and

handed Casper his phone back. "I'm... well, I'm sorry you got involved in all of this. I'm sure you had better things to do."

Casper grinned. I *wish I had better things to do.*

Daniel stepped towards his car and then turned back to Casper. "Oh, and your girlfriend called."

"Delaney?" Casper said. He loved the sound of her name on his lips.

"The Detective?" Daniel said.

"That's the one."

Daniel grinned. "She said you two need to talk."

CHAPTER FOUR

THE SCHOOL BELL rang and like one of Pavlov's test subjects, every student scurried into a nearby classroom like cockroaches in the midnight hour. Kyle Pittman watched the flood of teenage angst and hormones as they trickled into their desks and conversation hummed. A cloud of pungent perfume replaced the smell of dry erase markers. He liked that the students felt comfortable enough to talk freely to one another in his classroom. In his days as a student, he'd suffered under the ruthless reign of too many teachers who ruled with an iron fist. Who'd used fear as their means of keeping order. Instead, he did his best to mirror the educators that were human. Genuine. Authentic.

Kyle stood from his desk in the back of the classroom. The desk wobbled as he put his left palm on the surface to help his aching back. *Too many miles this morning, Kyle. Take it easy tomorrow.* The mental notes he made were all-too-often forgotten by the next morning. He'd hit the fork in the trail and always opt for another loop. There was something honorable about punishing his body. Pushing the limits. Never quitting. But none of that mattered to the gaggle of high school juniors that sat before him wiping the sleep from their eyes.

He cleared his throat and moved to the front of the classroom. The whiteboard had remnants of his previous lecture for the honors class yesterday. He often left the notes up to remind the other students how far ahead some of their peers were. They were busy preparing for the AP exams while this middle-of-the-road bunch fought through the end of *Of Mice and Men* and opening the pages of Mary Shelley's *Frankenstein*.

"Alright, settle now. Let's get started. I'd like a volunteer to discuss what they learned from their research on Mary Shelley."

A smattering of hands raised halfway in the air. Kyle had grown accustomed to this half-assed approach to participation. Only the overeager kids raised their skinny pencil arms straight in the air. Still, it was better than nothing.

"Kelsey, want to get us started?" Kyle said with his eyes on the iPad in front of him. He knew every student's name, but the lack of eye contact kept the element of surprise intact. Kelsey was notorious for smacking her gum in the middle of Kyle's lectures. A small price for her to pay for her shenanigans.

"Uh—Mr. Pittman, I didn't—" Kelsey fumbled for words like she was playing a game of hot potato.

"Alright, who *did* the research that was assigned for homework?" Nobody looked up. In his periphery, he saw hands raise. "Harrison?"

The red-headed boy resembled Kyle as a child. Embers for hair. Pale skin. More freckles than stars in the sky. "Sure! Mary Shelley was born in London. Published Frankenstein when she was twenty-one years old and didn't do too much else in her career." Harrison rushed through words like they were about to disappear from his brain. "I also read on Wikipedia that her idea for the novel came from a nightmare she had. Makes sense, you know?"

"Thanks, Harrison." Kyle forced a grin. "Now, I believe you went over the basics of different literature genres in your previous

English classes last year. Right?" Crickets chirped in some far-off distance. "Can anybody tell me what type of story Frankenstein is? No need to raise hands, just call out. Let's hear it."

"Fiction!" a small chorus of voices said.

"Okay, yes, but be more specific. What type of fiction?"

Hesitant voices shouted all sorts of words. *Old. English. Classic. Gothic.* Kyle shook his head. "Keep digging. What is this story truly about? Kelsey?"

Kelsey looked startled at the sound of her name twice in one day. She paused and looked at the drab book that sat on her desk on top of decades-old doodles and inscriptions.

"S-Science Fiction?"

"Bingo," Kyle exclaimed. "Kelsey is on top of it. And what about the story is scientific?"

"Well, I haven't read it all yet but—"

"Just from what you know. The story of Frankenstein is one of the most popular in the world. They have transformed it into many films and other works. Even without reading it, I'd surmise you know the premise."

"Surmise?"

"Assume."

"You know what they say happens when you assume Mr. P," Kelsey chuckled. Kyle went stone-faced.

"Never heard of it. But why science fiction?"

"Because like, the doctor takes a monster and makes it alive again. That's science to me."

"Excellent. And I know you all are into monsters. Vampires, Werewolves; all of that. This will be a fun one. Any questions? Anybody nervous to read a spooky story?" Heads nodded, and he dropped the subject. "Great. Great start class. Now I'd like you to break off into your quads and discuss what you learned about the author. I'll ask each pod to report out in twenty minutes."

The nails-on-chalkboard sound of metallic desk legs as they scraped against the scratched linoleum floor was nauseating but

19

short-lived. They broke off into their small groups. Kyle circled to ensure that each group was on task. Small group discussions too often led to in-depth analysis of pep rallies or somebody's awful haircut. Engagement was key. Plus, this was *Frankenstein*. The original monster story. The seed of them all.

After two laps, Kyle sat back at his desk and opened the bottom right drawer of his desk. He noticed the phone towards the bottom had a notification. He glanced around at the busy students, all diverging from the life story of Mary Shelley, and approaching the latest gossip. With their attention occupied, Kyle broke his cardinal rule for the students. He checked his phone.

A text popped up on his screen through WhatsApp. His palms were sweaty as he swiped it open. He read the instructions and surveyed the distracted class again as he archived the message. He swallowed the lump in his throat, shocked at how routine breaking the law had become.

For the rest of the period, Kyle half-heartedly led the class through exercises he'd pulled from the internet about Shelley's life and the misconceptions about Frankenstein as a novel. The bell rang and released Kyle from his misery. His heart wasn't in it anymore. His mind either. He daydreamed about cash that would soon deposit into his account. A lifelong vacation on a beach somewhere with little umbrellas in the drinks. Stunning women in little to no clothing. Just a little longer. So close.

Between classes, Kyle poked his head out and saw Andy in the hallway. He gave him a nod and Andy approached through a sea of acne-riddled faces and prepubescent voices that cracked as they discussed the latest memes on TikTok.

"Hiya, Coach Tucker," said one girl who had caked on way too much makeup.

"Hey there, Molly. Ready for the meet this weekend?" Andy said in his best authoritative voice. "Hillside High can run with the best of 'em this year."

"We'll take them down. We're deeper than we were last year.

Our top six cancels out their top-heavy seniors. Just you wait and see..." Molly reached out for a high-five and continued onward towards class.

"*Hiya, Coach Tucker,*" Kyle mimicked the young girl's voice.

"Mr. Pittman, a pleasure as always."

"Got a minute?" Kyle asked.

"You know it. I've got a work block. What's up?" Andy said.

Kyle nodded towards the door, and they slipped into Kyle's classroom. Stock posters of classic works of literature lined the walls. *The Catcher in the Rye. To Kill a Mockingbird. Death of a Salesman.* Crap leftover from past classrooms and hauled out of storage to decorate the tan cinderblock walls. Neither the students nor the teachers wanted to keep the prison-like aesthetic that an empty classroom came with. They stood in front of a *Great Gatsby* cutout peeling off the wall in one corner. Kyle pulled out his phone and showed Andy the message.

Andy grinned. "You're up. Son of a bitch."

Kyle nodded.

"Happy for you, bud. Have to say that I hoped to get a job soon." Andy rubbed his neck. "Regina is after me for alimony that she knows I don't have. She's ready to request full custody and all that. Tough times."

"Sorry, man." Kyle closed his phone. "I bet you'll get the next one and if not, I'll switch with you. Just gotta keep it on the down-low. I'm not trying to piss him off."

"Yeah, weird how we're still shaking in our boots, afraid of some asshole we've never met. But sometimes it's better to stay in the dark, you know what I mean?"

"That *asshole* has paid for your last two Disney vacations and my new car," Kyle laughed. "I'd rather be fearful and avoidant than risk pissing off some mob boss somewhere."

"You think he's in the mob?" Andy laughed. "Oh shit, like a career criminal? Like Tony Soprano or something?"

"Haven't given it much thought. The paychecks are fat. The

jobs are weird. But it's easy money. Beats the hell out of preaching about classic lit to a bunch of kids in suburbia."

"You mean they're easy for you." Andy glanced towards the door and then continued. "I had to bust my ass to get in decent enough shape to not look like a square peg next to a round hole out there."

"Metaphors are your strong suit, Andy," Kyle chuckled. "Tolkien has nothing on you."

"Thanks, teach." He approached the door. "Let me know how tomorrow goes, yeah?"

Kyle smiled. "If I make it out alive."

CHAPTER FIVE

LONGLEAF PINES STOOD in thickets and towered over Casper's car as he drove past the beloved Punkhorns. The sweet familiar smell of evergreens mixed with salty sea air reminded him of the hot summer months spent working on the case. Although it had left the town with more gossip than answers, Casper saw the case as a victory. After all, it brought Delaney Shepard into his life. Now, he just had to figure out how to keep her around.

He cruised past the turnoff for the public parking lot and sputtered up a steep hill that provided a magnificent view of Seymour Pond. Two blocks later, Casper veered up a gravel and seashell driveway. At the top, a gray-haired woman sat in a yellow Adirondack chair with a dog splayed out on the grass by her feet. She waved at Casper as he stepped out of his car.

"I think we finally found Hoagie's breaking point," Ann Peck said.

"Somehow, I doubt that. Frisbee?"

She shook her head. "Nope, we swam with him in the pond."

Casper leaned down and scratched behind his dog's ears. "Hoagie, do the words 'spoiled rotten' mean anything to you?"

Hoagie rolled onto his back, and Casper scratched his stomach. Few things were as inviting as a cute dog begging for a belly rub, even if the pup was a complete ham.

"Did you crack the case?" Ann asked.

Casper laughed. "In a way. It's out of my hands now, but I think Doris and Daniel Marsh will be just fine."

Ann smiled. "You know, if you ever decide the PI work isn't cutting it around here, we could use some help at the library."

"I appreciate it and will absolutely let you know. For now, I've got to go though. Hoagie, you ready?"

Ann rested her book on the arm of the chair and stood. Hoagie jumped and stretched with his front paws on her jeans. "Still heading out tomorrow?"

Casper nodded. "That's the plan. Although I just got a message that Delaney needs to talk to me, so I'm less certain than before."

Ann put a hand on his shoulder. "I'm sure it's just to plan your route south. Be excited. Meeting the parents is a big step."

"I'm well aware..."

"Being nervous is expected, but just be yourself. Be confident and approach it like a case. The case of the potential in-laws."

Casper raised his eyebrows.

"Too soon?"

Casper smiled. "Just a bit. It's only been a few months."

Ann shrugged. "Sometimes that's all that it takes."

"We'll see." She shook him off. "See you soon, Hoagie." She leaned down and held his face. "I'll work on my frisbee technique in the meantime."

After dropping Hoagie back at home, Casper made the quick drive over to the Brewster Police Station and parked in the lot next to the firehouse. He moseyed toward the front doors, reached for the handle and had to dive out of the way as they busted open. A scraggly-haired man shot out like a bullet. He cackled to himself and then met eyes with Casper.

"Free as a bird, once again!" the man shouted. Casper didn't have to look twice. He'd heard the stories of the infamous Morris Hanifin and had confirmed most of them by now. An officer smoked a cigarette next to a bench out front. He let out a groan and then nodded towards Morris. "See you soon, Hanifin."

Morris turned back with a grin that only a mother could love. "Not if I see you first!"

Inside the station, the air hung in the early autumn stage between heat and air conditioning. Stale coffee stung Casper's nostrils. He poked his head into the bullpen and caught Delaney's attention. She sat at her desk behind a mountain of file folders and papers that could give Everest a run for its money. She waved him over. He glanced around the room and tiptoed towards her.

"Casper?" A voice boomed out of the corner. Casper froze and turned his head to the left. A rotund man with one button misaligned on his uniform smiled at him. "Thought that was you."

"Chief, nice to see you."

"Staying out of trouble?" Chief Slimmer said. He leaned against the doorframe to his office, and Casper worried that the entire building may collapse under his weight.

"Yes, sir. Detective Shepard here makes sure of it."

Delaney looked up from her paperwork. "Who said he isn't in trouble right now?"

Slimmer raised his eyebrows, faked a wince, and then closed his office door. Casper sat in an orange vinyl chair next to her desk. "So, am I?"

Delaney grinned, scribbled on the top of a file, and closed it. "I am one day away from the longest vacation I've had since I joined the force."

"And I'm... excited to join you?" Casper asked.

"Is that a question? Are you now unsure of that?" Delaney's poker face could do damage in Vegas.

"No. Well... the question was actually if I'm still joining you."

She grinned. "Oh, you're coming. Can't get rid of me that easily. Mr. Kelly. But here I am, just minding my business today, so close to a vacation, as I may have mentioned, and I get a call about a creepy man outside of the WBCA building peering through windows."

Casper's cheeks turned cherry red. "I-"

"Look, Casper. If you're into older women exercising, the internet is a wonderful place for you." She smiled at him.

"I'll take your word for it."

"What was the case this time?"

"Doris Marsh."

Delaney chuckled. "Say no more. Everything work out okay?"

"Yep. Although, I'm not certain that she's still going to pay me. Could I hire you to shake her down for me?"

Delaney hesitated. "Can I ask a question as a detective and not as your girlfriend?"

"Uh oh."

"I'll take that as a yes."

"Sure, go for it."

"What is with these cases, Casper?"

"What do you mean?"

"When you got hired to come out here, you had this big reputation. Maybe I hadn't heard of you, but Ann Peck had. You were the legend. Solving the unsolvable. De-mystifying the paranormal theories of the world."

"And?"

"Then you come here and score a big win. I mean, a big one. Then you say you're going to hunker down in Brewster to write about it and flirt with me."

"I didn't realize—"

"Now, I'm not complaining about that. You delivered on the second half at least. But otherwise, you've been taking lame-duck cases that Nancy Drew could solve."

"Hey, don't knock Nancy Drew."

"I would never. But maybe it's time to step away from the Cape."

"Like on a road trip to meet your parents?"

"As a start, sure. When you come back, it may be time to take a good hard look at your prospects as a private investigator out here. May have to find you a new niche."

Casper smiled. "That's fair. Is that what you wanted to talk about?"

Delaney put both of her hands on the desk. "That and... how do you feel about splitting the drive up a bit? Stopping halfway. North Carolina."

"What's in North Carolina?"

"My cousin Zoe and her fiancé Gil."

"She's the park ranger?"

"That's the one. She's a delight. You'll love her. Plus, Gil is an oddball, so you two will get along perfectly."

"I'm game. Do you want me to look into hotels, or..."

"She's got a spare room. The park gives her a house to live in while she's working there. How cool is that? Maybe we both picked the wrong career."

Casper chuckled. "Can't wait. I'll see you tonight?"

"As long as you show up with Eggplant Parm from Three Kings, you may even get a kiss goodnight," Delaney said with a wink. "Get home and start packing. We hit the road in the morning."

A HALF HOUR LATER, Casper jogged up the creaky stairs that led to his crow's nest apartment over the Owl's Nest. The hustle of the daily coffee rush had died down, but the soothing tones of Coltrane still echoed through the speakers that sat just below his floorboards. *At least they have a flawless taste in music.*

Something sat jammed between Casper's door and the frame. He unlocked the door and a white envelope fell onto the ground before him. Hoagie burst through the door, armed with enough licks to melt down a lollipop. Casper scooped the note off the ground and turned it over as he gave Hoagie a belly rub. The front was blank. Inside, Casper found a note.

'She's not who you think she is,' the note said. 'Ask her about Raven Rock.'

CHAPTER SIX

THE SMELL of onions sizzling in olive oil wafted around the kitchen wall as Zoe kicked off her boots in the mudroom. She unhooked her utility belt and let it clunk on top of the wooden bench in the doorway. It had been a day like that. But cooked onions were a good sign. Gil knew food was her love language. They'd taken the quiz three times with no conclusion on his, but despite that, Zoe knew what made him tick. And it wasn't *only* scientific journals and research studies.

"Is that my paramour?" Gil shouted from the kitchen.

Zoe smiled. She slipped out of her light jacket, but her finger caught on the fabric. *Damn ring.* She moved the jacket sleeve off like it was an egg that might crack. *Sure is taking longer to get used to than those blog posts told me.* She kicked off her boots and strolled towards the kitchen. "Did they send the cute chef?" Zoe said.

The familiar notes of *"Lookin' Out My Backdoor"* greeted her just as warmly as the smells of Gil's cooking. "Unfortunately, they did not." Gil laughed. "You will have to settle for the nerdy one this time."

"Again? Aw, shucks," Zoe said with a grin. She sorted through bills and junk mail that was stacked on the coffee table. "Can I get a discount then? I specifically asked for the cute chef!"

Gil's voice grew louder as she strolled into the kitchen. "Will the promise of an extra slice of homemade pizza help? I was hoping for a generous gratuity this evening." He grinned in his navy blue apron.

Zoe let out a sigh as she slumped into Gil and he wrapped his arms around her. The embrace was warm. Familiar. She didn't want it to end.

"Another tough shift?" Gil asked, his accent at its strongest.

"More desk work. Less legwork. Same old sh—"

"I would estimate that desk work still beats sweeping floors or life as a sanitation engineer. Both of which sound preferable to me at the moment, considering my drudge…"

Zoe leaned against the counter as Gil turned on the oven light and checked on the crust. "I take it that your day of writing didn't go as planned?"

"I estimate I made one percent of progress." Gil held up his pointer finger. "Within a margin of error of my sampling, so it is not significant progress." A stray lock of his brown hair kept falling over the lines on his forehead, despite his constant head toss to keep it at bay.

"One percent every day adds up, Gil."

"Transition, did you know this song is about LSD?"

"Did you just announce a transition? Yes, Gil. We've been over this a hundred—"

Gil did his best Fogerty impression as he dropped the onions into the sauce and layered on mozzarella. *"Tambourines and elephants playing in the band. Won't you take a ride on the flying spoon?"*

Zoe kissed him to shut him up. "Stick to your day job. Leave the singing to the experts. Unless you're thinking of taking some LSD and writing some music?"

"After today, perhaps that would be wise."

"I want to hear more. I'm sure it wasn't that bad." Zoe headed towards the bedroom but shouted back. "Tell me about it after I change?"

Gil mumbled something as Zoe retreated into their cramped bedroom. The queen bed butted up against the two tiny nightstands that were wedged between two overstuffed dressers. They had kicked her beloved bookshelf to the curb, or more accurately, the shed in the backyard. She wrangled open the stubborn closet door, and the hinges let out a creak as they bent. The bare walls glared back at her as she changed.

A worn cardboard box collected dust at the end of the hallway, leftover from last year's move. Zoe skirted around it each time she stepped out of the room, similar to her handling of big life decisions. Thankfully, Gil had decided for the both of them when he didn't renew his lease. Most days, it felt like the right call.

Life as a lone wolf had been hard to walk away from, even with the promise of someday starting a pack. To family and friends, Zoe would cite Gil's flawless taste in music (and all things CCR) and his cute dimples as reasons to keep him around. Deep down, it was his patience. The man never rushed her. Even when it came to decorating, buying a new turntable, or starting a family.

Zoe tossed her uniform top onto the bed. The only signs of wear were from the flour on Gil's apron in the kitchen. She hung it back up in the closet, ready for another shift of paperwork tomorrow morning. The sight didn't match her vision for the job that she'd accepted six years ago. Back then, she'd expected to come home with dirt-caked boots that stunk to high heaven and a filthy uniform that served as a proud reminder of a hard day's work. Instead, she could almost make out creases in her pants from sitting on her ass all day.

Gil sang along to a Paul Simon record. Flour fingerprints on the plastic turntable display case looked like a crime scene that had been dusted for prints. Back in the kitchen, Cecilia was breaking Gil's heart. That told her all she needed to hear. He'd had a decent day. Zoe had learned to understand the swings that Gil had as a struggling researcher, author, and aspiring podcaster. She'd nodded and grinned through many early drafts of chapters and episodes. It was a relief that she didn't wake up with a sore neck. Gil never flinched when she vented about her monotonous days at work, so Zoe mirrored it back to him when he needed that support. She aimed to be his beacon of encouragement. Lighthouse in a storm. His biggest cheerleader, even if there wasn't enough money in the world to convince her to don the pom-poms and skirt.

Gil pulled a steaming pizza topped with caramelized onions, cremini mushrooms, and red bell peppers out of the oven. Early on, Zoe longed for meat, particularly bacon, but soon grew to appreciate Gil's vegetarian habits. It didn't hurt that he did the lion's share of the cooking.

"Looks delicious, dear," Zoe smiled.

"Capsicum, er, Peppers are leftovers from the garden. The last from our summer harvest, I believe. We should triple our seeds next year." Gil scribbled a note on the magnetic whiteboard on the fridge.

Zoe nodded and plopped herself into the wooden chair next to the kitchen table. A tan table cloth decorated with forest green pine trees stuck to her elbows as she hung her head and wallowed in self-pity. Gil examined her like an animal in a lab. "I sense that you either partook in a midday fast or are demonstrating the physical symptoms of stress."

She shot him a look.

"Noted." He smiled. "I once again have let the inner scientist in me emerge. No more examinations."

She pulled her head out of her hands. "Anyway, tell me about your day. Give me some good news."

"Nothing remarkable happened. The progress I made in the morning was encouraging. One thousand and nine hundred new words on the page. I celebrated my minor victory with a jaunt down Sycamore Trail before the rain moved in." Gil tossed a slice onto his plate and sat. "Along the way, I mentally revised what I had written. By the time my alarm sounded to start dinner, I had whittled my progress down to a mere three hundred and seven words."

"Hey, that's great! Step by step, right? That's three hundred and seven more words than yesterday."

"I believe we may need to revise that phrase to 'inch by inch' but yes, it is progress."

"Why do you seem hesitant to celebrate this?" Zoe rolled the pizza cutter through the pie and slid a steaming slice onto her plate.

"I have been pondering topics for season two."

Zoe frowned. *Not this again.* "I am under specific instructions from Past Gil to remind you that you need to finish your manuscript before writing anything for season two of the podcast."

Gil grinned. "Yes, my arch-nemesis, Past Gil. What a deplorable," he said. He joined her at the table and stared at his pizza. "What a deplorable."

"Want to hear what present Zoe thinks?"

"Always."

Zoe blew on her pizza to cool it down. "She believes you should work on whatever you need to. But she also believes that if you need more time on the manuscript, you should give your editor a heads up. You know?"

Gil nodded and took a bite. He shot his mouth open and steam escaped. He waved at his mouth with his hand to waft cool air his way. Zoe chuckled at the scene and took a big bite of her own.

"Men are such babies with temperatures," she said.

"I hate to think that my entire gender is being brought down by my inadequate abilities to handle the heat. Perhaps we could do some research."

"Yeah, you definitely have room on your plate for that. It can go right between your podcast and your manuscript."

"Curious minds, Zoe. Anyhow, more desk duty? I recall Joanne was returning from vacation soon."

Zoe shrugged. "No clue. Maybe tomorrow. But hopefully, with the time that I committed there this week, I will be exempt for the next month and a half." She tucked a stray strand of blond hair behind her ear. "Hell, I'd take a shift cleaning bathrooms with the maintenance crew before I'd go back to that rickety old chair."

"You can start with ours," Gil said with a grin.

Zoe finished her first slice and reached for another. "This is delicious as always, dear. Did you use basil from the garden too?"

Gil nodded and mumbled something inaudible.

"We did have one minor event that may interest you though," Zoe said. "But I'll only share it if you promise not to make a big fuss."

"Lay it on me, Ranger Watts."

"Two kids reported another sighting."

Gil dropped his pizza to his plate and stared at her. "And you did not lead with this the second you walked in?"

"I didn't want—" Before Zoe could finish, Gil had sprinted out of the kitchen. Seconds later, he returned. He was out of breath and carried a cork-board with papers that hung off of it in scattered directions. An Umstead State Park map was pinned to the surface. A handful of red and yellow pins dotted the vast acres of the park.

Gil pointed to the map. "Where?"

Zoe let out a sigh and kept her eyes on her pizza. "Off the fishing trail that bisects the main trail by Big Lake."

Gil traced his finger over the trail and found the hand-drawn addition to the map. "Here?" Gil pointed a few feet west from the large body of water labeled *Big Lake*.

Zoe had always mocked the inventiveness of the park staff that had named the body of water. "They were fishing there but saw it further down the trail. Fifty yards at least. But Gil they were teenagers, it could be some stupid prank or maybe they know about the reported sightings."

Gil scratched his chin, then shook his head. "Seems to be a peculiar prank for teenagers. I will mark it down."

He added a tack to the map, propped the corkboard up on the counter, and stepped back to examine the data. Zoe rolled her eyes and brought her plate to the sink. As she wiped it clean, she looked back to see Gil carry the map back into the living room. Zoe put away the leftovers and joined him. She let herself sink into the couch.

"What is the pulse of the rangers? Is Mathias—"

"He's still Mathias. Nobody seems to think twice about any of it." Zoe turned on the TV. "They all just say it's people seeing what they want to see. What's that called again?"

"Confirmation bias. It is unclear if it applies to this case though. Typically, it fits with—"

"Nobody seems inclined to do anything besides take a lazy drive by with a truck if the location is convenient." Zoe fiddled with the remote. "We're still pinning them to the map like you are, but that's where it stops. Although, I think I saw Clem taking pins off the map the other day."

Gil shook his head. "There is always a non-believer in the bunch. They are hard-pressed to take action. A significant development may do the trick. But action will be difficult to force." Gil mumbled to himself as he looked at the map. "Perhaps a nudge from a government official. Perhaps a photograph as evidence. Or perhaps an attack."

"Yeah, that sounds about right. Although, personally, I just want this to be over." Zoe sighed. "We're so close to winter. Shorter hours and fewer visitors in the park. I can almost smell it." Zoe clicked on their Recently Watched queue. "Anyway, did you want to try and finish that documentary or—"

"No TV for me tonight. This has my full attention," Gil said with his eyes fixed on the map.

Zoe rolled her eyes. *I'm playing second fiddle to hairy beasts again.* "Well, I'm going to watch *Longmire* reruns until I pass out then. Come get me from the couch when you go to bed?"

"Of course, dear." Gil kissed her on the cheek and scurried off with a newfound enthusiasm to his office.

Zoe grinned and let her mind wander off as a tenacious team of Sheriff's deputies investigated crimes in Wyoming. For the time being, fiction was far more interesting than the boring reality that had become her life.

CHAPTER SEVEN

THE DAWN CHORUS reached its crescendo as Kyle drove. Daylight was dim behind the horizon. Mockingbirds and bluebirds sung their finest soundtrack songs. Dew clung to blades of grass. Droplets had begun to evaporate in the rising temperatures of the morning hour, but many remained nonetheless. The slam of the car's trunk lid echoed and bounced off the maze of pine trees that bordered the illegal parking spot. Kyle glanced around, but there wasn't another soul in sight. He tossed the backpack over his shoulder.

He jumped back into his car, drove another mile toward the entrance gate of the park, and cruised into a vacant spot between two other cars. Each had empty bike racks and bumper stickers from various marathons and triathlons. A not-so-subtle signal to onlookers that they were active and fit. Like a patch on a backpack in junior high.

Kyle pulled his car key off the ring, wove the drawstring of his shorts through the keyhole, tied a knot, and tossed the rest of his keys into his center console. He slung the backpack straps over his arms. It hung too high on his back, so he dropped the shoulders down and connected the front buckle over his chest to prevent it from bouncing along as he jogged.

A split-rail fence made of cedar and ash marked the edge of the park property, but a path with well-worn tread led around the edge. He cleared the security measure with ease. Posts that marked each segment of fence splintered beside marks from a creature's gnawing that scarred the bottom.

Pine needles crunched beneath his running shoes, the give and take of each needle bracing together with every step. A tenderness in his knee ached with the first few steps, but he transitioned into a jog before long. One foot in front of the other. A cyclist whirred past and dove down the driveway. Kyle veered off the main road and onto the trails. Pine trees bracketed the path. Scrape marks from a buck rub scarred the trunk of a red oak to the side. Rhododendrons nodded along in the breeze with their familiar waxy leaves. Soil mixed with fallen leaves and seeds dropped from gum trees along the path. The smooth introductory tones of Nina Simone's *Sinnerman* blared through Kyle's headphones as he started at a steady pace as he passed the entrance gate.

The forest thickened, and shadows appeared in the last traces of moonlight. There was always something special about dawn. The fresh day still finding its footing. Sunlight on the horizon, just out of reach. Birdsong was a backbeat to the rhythmic thump of feet on the trail.

His cushioned soles supported him as he drove his knees upward and climbed the first hill of the day. His lungs burned from the cold air that marked an autumnal Carolina morning. Sweat beaded on his brow. A drop trickled down his forehead and tickled his skin like a crawling ant. The weight of the bag dug the straps into his shoulders, so he tightened the chest clip and took some pressure off.

Within thirty minutes, Kyle had cruised into the depths of the park and turned onto the shortcut trail, *his* shortcut trail, which had taken shape after countless trips. Rangers had stacked logs and debris over the beginning, but Kyle hurdled over them and continued onward. He grinned at the recent additions to the obstruction, constantly built up wider and taller, as if there wasn't always a way around. The rangers failed to respect Kyle's determination. Plus, the shortcut bisected the park and stripped at least twenty minutes off his round trip time. Better than that; it was empty. There were no joggers out for their morning miles or dog walkers holding their leash tight as their puppy snarled. Kyle's only company was nature. The birds in the trees. The tread on the trail. The still air mixed with morning sunshine.

Ten years and twenty pounds ago, Kyle would have said he could carry on for another hour without a break. His mind often flashed back to his moments of glory on the track. Diving across finish lines after the rubbery surface had rubbed his feet raw inside his flimsy track spikes. Friends and family cheering him on from uncomfortable aluminum bleachers. Teammates shouting out splits with each lap that he completed. The feverish excitement that would course through his veins upon hearing the official ring the bell for the final lap. The last fourhundred meters where everything hurts and nothing is easy. He'd leave it all on the track. His lungs on fire, but his legs carrying him through. Through, past the faded line on the surface that marked his end. His triumph. His trophy.

There were no moments where his teammates carried him off the field or when the crowd chanted his name. Track and field wasn't that kind of sport. Neither was cross-country. No, that type of reaction was fit for Olympians and world record holders, not middle-sized-state-college superstars that were, at best, the top runners in their counties. Maybe their state.

Instead, he basked in the glow of moments that were less than spectacular from the outside. Rowdy laughter on the team bus on the way home from a meet. Fast food trays covered with burgers and fries that toppled over as they moved. Hotel room shenanigans on road trips. The alluring look of a girl as he jogged past her on campus. Pasta parties where ten pounds of spaghetti would get wolfed down in the drop of a hat. Walking off their overstuffed guts on familiar trails that wove through peach orchards and family farms. A silent bond that didn't need formal recognition or naming. A brotherhood of sorts that made the misery of training and running a little more bearable. Some things were more meaningful than the numbers on a stopwatch.

Years stretched after graduation and much like Kyle's knees, most of the ties to that brotherhood grew weak. Strained by distance and time. Left instead with hurried moments of after-work happy hours and run clubs at breweries. FaceTime reunions and "we should catch up sometime!" on every birthday. It wasn't equivalent to the joy he once felt. But he'd kept running. Lower mileage. Slower times. More pain. His legs were sturdy, but the tendons ached each morning. Another sign of life passing him by.

Kyle slowed to a walk and took off his headphones. In college, such a break would earn a loud boo from his teammates. In those days, he would eventually give in and run with a forced grin. Not anymore. Now, he stood still and listened to the trees as they performed their swaying dance in the breeze. A scampering animal rustled leaves in the distance. An easy sound to distinguish from human footsteps. There were no humans around. The only other sound Kyle could hear was his heart thumping in his chest. Nerves and fatigue often came on with similar symptoms.

Your body doesn't tell you when you're out of shape. It happens like a river wearing down its banks. The body looks the same, but it's changed. The force of that flowing water has weakened. There's less blood pumping. Lactic acid becomes an all-too-familiar friend. Muscles ache in areas that you didn't know could ache. Early morning steps out of bed become reminders of every year you've lived. Of every mile you've run. Of every pounding your foot has taken against the pavement along the way. Age had a cryptic way of sneaking up on a person, every time your birthday neared like an annoying neighbor who seems to inch their house closer.

Kyle eyed the spot. He dropped to a knee and reached around the base of a moss-covered log that had fallen across the path. Ants crawled and fled the scene like a guilty party. He reached for the small latch under the natural camouflage of the greenery and flipped it open. The top of the log rose like an opening treasure chest. Creaked like a car door in desperate need of oil. The insides were bare, as they always were when Kyle arrived. He dropped the backpack into the log, lowered the top, re-locked the latch, and stood back up.

On the route back, Kyle let his mind wander back to the beach. His soon-to-be home. The sandy soil that mixed with the debris on the surface of the trail reminded him of warm summer days in the Outer Banks. Reminded him of the surprise on his friend's faces when he told them he'd rented everybody a house for a week. The looks that the women shot him after he told them about his side hustle that brought in extra dough. The brief, fleeting joy that came from that break from reality. The harsh return to the world that awaited him back home.

In moments of doubt, Kyle reminded himself. There was an endgame. A target set of numbers that were his ticket out. A net worth in his bank account that would justify the means. No more students who don't give a shit about literature. No more crappy teacher benefits. No more eleven-hour days at a school that smelled like old erasers and bleach. None of that would matter.

He dreamt of how his friends would react when they learned that he'd split town. His co-workers would gossip. Assume he lost his mind or went back to live with his parents. After all, no profession is more criminally underpaid than teachers. They'd emphasize the underpaid part and assume he fell on hard times. Nobody would take a second to re-examine the sentence. *Criminally underpaid.*

CHAPTER EIGHT

THE SUN SNUCK over the horizon as Delaney turned off of the Bourne Bridge and steered South away from Cape Cod. The butterflies that tickled Casper's stomach faded as they made their way through Rhode Island and into Connecticut. Conversation was light, and the playlist he had made for the occasion struck a chord with his co-pilot. Delaney was in a playful mood. Before long, he almost forgot about the ominous note buried inside his duffel bag.

The internet provided little clues to what the cryptic message could mean. The first part was clear enough. Delaney was hiding something. That didn't bother Casper. Everybody had secrets. Monsters in their closet. Demons that they wrestle with when they're alone. Hell, Casper had just come to see the edge of relief from crippling claustrophobia although he had a long way to go. *Who am I to talk?*

The added mystery was that aside from the note, Delaney seemed like an open book. She was transparent and direct. Never one to shy away from what she meant or wanted. But that all made sense in its own way. If she had something to hide, there was likely a damn good reason for it. That made his internal debate even more difficult.

95 South looked like a parking lot. Hoagie curled up in a ball on the back seat and snored the day away. Casper watched their arrival time tick up from mid-afternoon into the early evening hours. The scenery grew bland. Exit signs and rest stops repeated and blurred together. After a three-hour stretch where Casper's mind echoed with the words *Raven Rock*, Delaney pulled into a scenic overlook that overlooked nothing but office buildings. She returned from the tiny crowded bathrooms and encouraged Hoagie as he searched for an ideal spot to pee.

"Where are we?" Casper asked.

"Connecticut. Your turn!"

She tossed him the keys. Casper shrugged. "It all looks the same to me."

Delaney smiled. "Just keep it under one hundred, okay?"

Traffic cleared just south of the Tappan Zee Bridge. Delaney fiddled with her phone in the passenger seat. "You sure you're alright with whatever I choose?"

"Gimme your worst, Del," Casper said with a grin.

The speakers crackled and after ominous notes of a homemade theme song created on a synthesizer, a smoky voice with a thick British accent introduced the show.

"Welcome to another episode of The Elusive Beast. I am your host, Gil MacDougal. Today, we shall dive into the history of our beloved creature. Some mistakenly know it as Sasquatch. Others have labeled it a Yeti. But we know and will refer to our furry friend as Bigfoot."

"I did *not* take you as a Bigfoot truther, Delaney Shepard," Casper laughed.

"Give it a listen, will ya?"

"In the early afternoon of Friday, October 20th, 1967, Roger Patterson and his friend Bob Gimlin were riding northeast on horseback on the east bank of Bluff Creek, just northwest of Orleans, California and thirty-eight miles south of the Oregon border. After stopping for lunch, they

continued onward, and around one-thirty in the afternoon, they came to an overturned tree with a large root system. The downed tree sat at a turn in the creek and they described it as being 'nearly as tall as a living room'. They rounded it and spotted a figure behind the tree that was crouching down just to their left. Gimlin stood in pure shock. Patterson was awestruck. He tried to size up the creature with his eyes. He surmised it was at least seven feet tall. Standing on two feet. Bipedal. Apelike. Dark reddish-brown fur covering most of its body. Prominent breasts. It turned and saw them."

"Is this going to turn into some fetish thing? I've never heard somebody talk about Bigfoot's breasts with a straight face before. Who is this clown?" Casper said.

"Well, you can ask about that detail yourself."

Casper raised his eyebrows.

Delaney turned the phone his way. The podcast logo was the profile of a man looking off into the wilderness. "This is Zoe's fiancé, Gil."

"This is the same Gil? Oh, I'm sorry I said anything, I—"

"No, you're not wrong and this is nothing new. Zoe's heard it all. But she loves him anyway."

"Where's he from?"

"Outside of London. In the country. I forget the name but something ending in 'shire."

"Interesting. Okay, I'll keep an open mind. Let's hear some more. Maybe it gets better."

Delaney pressed play.

"Patterson grabbed his camera and started filming. They were over twenty-five feet away, but got footage of the creature walking away from them. He looked at Gimlin, who stood in pure shock, and then grabbed for his gun and ran after the creature. Within seconds of following, they had lost the creature's trail. It was nowhere to be found. They hurried home and reviewed the footage. They called in local researchers to show what they had found. A female ape-like creature that was taller and steadier on two feet than any they had ever heard of. They left

convinced they had captured indisputable evidence that Bigfoot did indeed exist."

Once the advertisement started, Casper provided a review. "He's a natural storyteller. That's a fact. I am the furthest thing from a Bigfoot believer, but he's got my attention."

"You don't buy into any of that? Mr. Paranormal Investigator?"

"Bigfoot isn't paranormal, and neither is my work. You know that's just a gimmick from the past. I guess I could see a world where he exists—"

"Or she. Breasts, Casper. Prominent breasts."

Casper turned red as a tomato. "Press play before I get more uncomfortable."

"This infamous film, which you in all likelihood have seen, lasts less than thirty seconds. The creature walks with ease away from the camera, turns to glare at the men, and then continues onward. Certain details were baffling to the experts. How did it evade their pursuit when they went to follow? Why did the creature have breasts when all reported sightings in the past were of male Bigfoots? What was the speed of the capture setting on the camera? More questions than answers surfaced."

"And we like Gil, yes?" Casper asked.

"He's a kook, but he's a lovable one. Just wait and see. He'll win you over within minutes. I get why Zoe is with him."

"Has she dated guys like him in the past?"

"She's got a string of poor choices and mistakes in her past, just like most of us. She was big on the dating apps for a while but said she found all the guys too boring."

"So, how did she meet Mr. Bigfoot?"

"He was doing research in the park. I think for a different project. Before all of this Bigfoot stuff became his focus. He stopped to ask her for directions and they got to talking."

"Guess he's a smooth talker then."

"Don't worry, he's got nothing on you," Delaney grinned. "It didn't hurt that they had two big things in common. First, they both have an annoying appreciation for Jim Carrey movies. If I had a nickel for every time that Zoe made me sit through *Dumb and Dumber* with her, I'd be retired and then some."

"Is this a bad time to admit that I love *Dumb and Dumber?*" Casper said.

"There's no good time to say that, so I'll just pretend you're making a joke. Anyway, the second was an undying love for Creedence Clearwater Revival."

"The band from the seventies?"

"That's the one. Zoe's a strange bird, but she's one of a kind. My take is that if Gil is all right by her, he's all right by me."

"Fair enough. I'm open-minded."

"Just don't quote Jim Carrey movies if I'm still in the room," Delaney said with a chuckle. "Anyway, let's see how this episode wraps up..."

"In recent years, experts have largely discredited the film. People have come forward claiming they made the suit that they wore. People have come forward saying that Patterson himself was in on the hoax. Others say that none of that matters because Patterson accomplished his goal. He made the study of Bigfoot a workable occupation. He opened the doors to let science in. Explore more with me the rest of this season as we dive further into the makings of this legendary beast. Next week, we will hear an interview with legendary cryptozoologist Grover Krantz and discuss the implications of his research. In the meantime, if you want to get a jump-start on the curriculum, you can pre-order my book, The Elusive Beast, on Amazon and at your local bookstore today. Until next time, I am Gilbert MacDougal. Stay safe, folks."

Spooky tones played over the credits. "Okay, that wasn't too bad. I didn't know he was promoting a book. That somehow makes it better," Casper said.

"I believe the book is still being written."

"Ah, so at least we've got that in common."

"Yeah, how's that coming along? Any agents knocking down your door to hear the story of The Punkhorns?"

"Not that I'm aware of. My old agent from the first book is out of the business. Apparently writing books is a less than viable way to make a living these days."

"Don't mention that to Gil."

"Oh, there are more than a few things I will not mention to Gil, but I'm still excited to meet him. Maybe more than ever before."

"Well, hope you are also ready for a slew of questions from Zoe. Nothing will be off-limits for her. She'll poke and prod. Ask you if you've ever been in love or what your deepest, darkest secret is. Be ready."

Deepest, darkest secret. Casper cracked his knuckles.

"Bring it on."

Lost in the brief distraction that Bigfoot provided, Casper swallowed the thought and decided that he'd let Delaney have her space. She'd bring it up in time. When it was natural. When it was right. He had earned her confidence. In time, she would reveal her secrets and they'd deal with the fallout. *She's not who you think she is.* When had that ever been a good thing?

CHAPTER NINE

THE SMELL of coffee woke Zoe from her fitful sleep. She blinked her eyes open, surprised to see that Gil had already left their bed. An email marked urgent blinked on her phone screen. She read through it and collapsed back onto the pillow. Work beckoned. Even on days off.

Gil entered their bedroom with a steaming mug of black coffee and a childish grin. "Your daily jolt of trimethylxanthine, dear."

Zoe shot him a playful look, and he placed the mug on her dresser. She hiked up her thick green uniform pants and kissed him on the cheek. "Thank you. Early morning motivation?"

"Just getting a jump on the day." He eyed her as she dressed. "I thought you closed today?"

Zoe buttoned the rest of her top and followed Gil into the kitchen. "I do, but Mathias called an all-staff. Have to leave in a few to get to the other side of the park." She noticed disheveled papers all over the kitchen table. "What'd you get into last night?"

He scrambled to organize them and carried the stack out of the room without a word. Zoe grabbed a granola bar out of the pantry and sipped the coffee he had made. She nearly spit it out. The taste was somewhere between boiled lemons and battery acid. Gil, who had more degrees than a thermometer, had yet to master the art of the pour-over and never failed to create a bitter concoction that Zoe worried would soon make the paint peel. She sipped a bit and heard him approaching, so she threw half of the mug down the drain.

"Is it better today?" He asked with a smile.

"It's great, Gil. Thanks for making me a cup. What did you get into last night? I didn't even hear you come to bed."

"I had an idea that I wanted to explore. I am hoping to let it guide me today." He kissed her on the cheek. "I am sorry if I woke you this morning."

"No bother. It's always nice to spend a little time with you in the morning before I head off on duty. Much better than a rushed dinner before mindless TV and falling asleep on the couch," Zoe said. She hugged him and finished the last of her granola bar. "Anyway, I'm off. Can't wait to hear what the day has in store for me."

"You never know; today may surprise you!" Gil shouted as she stepped out the door.

Zoe whizzed past the gates that once marked the entrance to Reedy Creek State Park. When Umstead State Park opened in 1937, government officials split the vast acreage into two, each named after a creek that ran through the grounds. Some thirty years later, state officials combined the land into one expansive park named after the esteemed Senator-cum-Governor William Bradley Umstead.

Her extended commute to the visitor's center was an unwelcome reminder of the size of the forest, which sat just under six thousand acres. Although Zoe's cottage on the quiet side of the park provided peace and tranquility, it also added a twenty-minute commute through twisty horse trails that were often flooded with oblivious cyclists. All that just to clock in for the day. Often, it was the only time she spent in the woods at all.

Aside from the rangers, the parking lot next to the Visitor's Center sat empty. Zoe parked next to the other white North Carolina State Parks trucks, surprised to see that she was the last to arrive. Clem Jenkins had an untouchable reputation as the last-person-to-show, and it was worrisome that even he had arrived before her.

The cramped conference room was the only meeting space that fit the entire staff. Stuffed to the gills with furniture and an over-sized table donated after renovations overhauled IBM's headquarters just down the road. Mathias sat at the head of the table, looking like a CEO who decided to play dress up and opted for the muted tans and greens of a Park Ranger uniform. His mustache, greased down at the ends, pressed into his cheeks like the Monopoly man. The cracked skin on his knuckles remained as a relic of time spent in the field. Chestnut hair covered most of his head, although it had continued to thin in the years since Zoe had started at the park. He looked as he usually did. Stoic.

To his left sat the ever-unreliable Clem Jenkins. Clem grinned from ear to ear as Zoe entered. She fought off her schoolyard instincts and kept her tongue inside her cheek. She poured a cup of coffee to help mask the persistent taste of Gil's sludge. The office's coffee was nothing to write home about either, but it didn't have the same chemical composition as paint thinner, so Zoe could gulp it down. She slid her plain white porcelain mug onto the table and glanced over at the last member of their team.

Ernest Henley's years as a high-ranking member of the Raleigh Police Department were his favorite and quite possibly only conversation topic. That and his time as a medic in the Army. Zoe had respect for the man's career achievements but often wanted to tell him to go yell it on the mountain each time he had her ear. His rants were famous amongst the staff and ranged from the medical inaccuracies of *M.A.S.H.* to how the Yankee transplants from the north were transforming Raleigh into Manhattan with their yuppie tendencies. Grumpy from Snow White would seem like a peach compared to old Ernest.

Ernest left the police force and after one year of retirement took an 'easy' job, as he put it, and joined the team of rangers that patrolled the grounds of Umstead State Park. Mathias carried a certain reverence for Ernest's military and police experience and often let him have the pick of the litter when the projects for the week came to light.

"Okay, let's get this over with," Mathias said. He glanced at his staff with a blank expression. "To be direct, my hand has been forced." He said each word like somebody held cue cards up for him. "State leadership has diagnosed our recent rash of peculiar activity as a problem. They tasked us with taking action."

"Action?" Clem laughed. "What in the heck does that mean?" His southern voice moved as slow as molasses.

"He wants us to hunt it," Ernest said. He tapped the butt of his gun. "Leave it to me; I'll take out our visitor. Friend or foe."

Clem pulled a toothpick from his mouth. "There ain't no visitor, Ernest. This is all a bunch of malarkey. What's that the kids say these days? Fake news?" He grinned at his attempt at youthful humor.

Mathias cleared his throat. "I am looking for something that will appease the upper management. Not something expensive, dangerous, or that could leave the door open for more of this bullshit down the road."

Zoe opened her mouth to speak, but Ernest interrupted before a sound could emerge. *What was that saying Joanne liked to use? Put enough men in a room and sure enough, they'll talk over themselves until the dogs come home.*

"How about a trap?" Ernest asked.

"Yeah." Clem faked a laugh. "Let's set a trap in our park. Brilliant plan, you snake in the grass. Do you want to call the state

51

attorney and explain our side of the lawsuit now, or wait until someone gets hurt?"

Mathias raised his hand and silenced the others.

Clem pushed on anyway. "Hey Mathias, what caused all of this anyhow?"

"There has been information shared and we—"

"I've been running all over hell's half acre lately, trying to get the trails in shape. I don't have a second to spare for this boondoggle," Clem said.

"Somebody made a convincing case to the authorities. Somebody anonymous," Mathias said with a glance towards Zoe.

"So, we just make a tip of our own that the whole thing was a hoax. Easy as pie," Clem said.

Mathias glared at him. Clem recoiled in his seat. "Zoe, thoughts on the matter?" Mathias said.

Zoe exhaled and stared at the table. "I'd imagine that we need to educate the public. Safely. Without causing a scene. Maybe we put up some posters with information about what to do when you see a bear or other—"

"Bear? There ain't no bears in suburban North Carolina, Hun," Clem laughed.

"Don't you *Hun* me. I'm suggesting that we—"

"Cheap and friendly to the public. Let's pencil that in." Mathias Wittles, ever the wordsmith. "Is that all?"

"What about game cameras?" Zoe asked.

"Oh, that's actually a great idea." Clem snapped his fingers. "We could put some up in the abandoned structures next to the Bike and Bridle Trail parking lot too. If I have to clean up one more piece of litter, I will-" He curled his hand into a fist.

"I could put some in the areas where we've seen a cluster of sightings. Maybe we can wrap this up by tomorrow morning and ease their minds." Zoe's mind pictured a long day in the woods, climbing trees and positioning the game cameras at just the right angle.

Mathias pondered the idea. He nodded. "Simple enough. We already have the cameras, right Ernest?"

Ernest stood. "We have some in the closet from the wild boar incident last year. I believe it'll send any photos taken directly to the park email address." He nodded towards the closet. "They will capture anything that moves, so we may get a bunch of deer, fox and squirrel, but it may appease the powers that be." Ernest spoke to Mathias like nobody else was in the room.

"Good." Mathias nodded. "Dismissed."

Zoe moved toward the closet, but Mathias' voice interrupted her halfway. "Ernest will set up the cameras. Zoe, I need you on the desk for the morning. Joanne will be back from vacation this afternoon."

Her heart sank faster than a penny in a wishing well. She nodded and retreated to the lobby before anyone could see the disappointment on her face. Mathias followed and stood over her. The tension was palpable. Zoe braced for the worst. He played with his mustache for a second until Zoe noticed his stare and put two and two together.

"Sir, I had nothing to do with the anonymous tip. I swear to you. I'd never—"

Mathias raised his hand. "I know it wasn't you."

As he turned away, Zoe caught half of a smile on his face. Once he left, Zoe faced the stark reality of the moment. Only one person outside of that conference room had the knowledge and motive to call in such a tip.

Jesus, Gil. What in the hell were you thinking?

CHAPTER TEN

ANDY KNOCKED a cigarette out of the half-empty pack and into his palm. He played with it for a second, rolling it back and forth between his fingers like a carnival trick.

"You ever smoke, Kyle?"

"Cigarettes? No." Kyle kicked at a rock on the ground. "Weed. Yes."

"Cigarettes are a hell of a vice." Andy put one into his mouth. "I've quit more times than I'd like to admit, but that's a curse I share with half of this country."

"That a verifiable stat?"

"Sure as shit is. What else do you think half this country has in common? Smoking crosses political lines. Geographical borders. There isn't much that we as folks have in common but damn it if we don't all have our vices."

A bell rang at an ear-piercing volume throughout the school. They both ignored it.

"Fair enough. You selling tobacco on the side now?"

Andy continued on. "I once justified the *just one more* thought by thinking of all the farmers around the Carolinas that made their riches off tobacco crops back in the day."

"Mhm. Tobacco Road and all that jazz." Kyle glanced at his watch.

"All that jazz." Andy chuckled. "Hell, they built this entire region on tobacco. James Buchanon Duke founded Duke University with his earnings from the old Bull Durham company."

"Thought that was a baseball team?"

"One day, they just decided that they're proud of it. Opted to keep the old-fashioned billboards up as a reminder to the dark days of segregation, tobacco farming and greed. Shit is wrong."

"Didn't hear the bell ring and start my own personal history class, Coach Tucker."

Andy fumbled for a light. A stiff wind rounded the corner of the parking lot and wiped out the flickering flame he'd pulled close to his mouth. He used another hand to shield his cigarette from the elements and took a long drag.

"Between all that and the history of prohibition down here, not much has changed," Andy continued. "Our cars got faster, the drugs grew more dangerous, and we got better at hiding things. That's how."

"How what?"

"How I sleep at night." Andy smiled. "I tell myself that our ancestors did the same shit we're doing these days to earn a buck. Probably on the same property that we've made our own little smuggling playground."

A student pushed open the exit door, saw the two teachers outside, and spun back into the building. Kyle waited until they were alone.

"A means to an end." Kyle chuckled. "I'm in the same boat, so I don't know why you're trying to convince—"

"Man, there ain't no boat. The only person I'm trying to convince here is myself. How do *you* carry on knowing inside that you're as corrupt as sin when the price is right?"

"It's just drugs." Kyle shrugged and stepped away from the cloud of smoke from Andy's puff. "They'd find a way to the pockets they end up in. I'm just a cog."

"In more ways than one."

"Hell, so are you, man. We're nothing. If we dropped dead on a Friday, The Fox would have a new runner in place by Monday."

"More like Friday night, but thanks for the reassurance, bud."

"I've got to run. Office hours and whatnot," Kyle said and turned toward the door.

Andy kept his eyes on the sea of cars parked in the lot. "I've got a job."

Kyle raised his brow. "About time."

"I'm hungry for it, so, of course I get a job the day that I'm supposed to take my god-damned kids to Carowinds." Andy shouted. "Talk about some luck." His hair looked unkempt. The red in his eyes were classic insomniac. Or Andy had, as threatened, picked up an extra shift as a nighttime security guard somewhere to keep himself out of the red.

"I'm sorry, dude. I—"

Andy raised his hand. "None of that pity. Just let me bitch. How was the last job?"

"Easy as ever. But the bag was heavier than last time."

"Yeah, been there. I think The Fox has been taking it easy on me. Giving me lighter loads. Started heavy, but it's lighter as of late." Andy laughed. "Maybe he somehow knows that my knees are shot. Maybe my doctor is The Fox."

"Maybe you're just getting stronger. Ever think of that, man?"

Andy belly-laughed. "Shit, when you approach forty, nothing inside you is getting stronger except a sense that you screwed your entire life up. The only direction my body is trending is downward. I appreciate the kind words though. You think you'd be up to take one for the team tomorrow?"

Kyle hesitated. "I'm still trying to—"

"I know, I know. Rules say it's once a week and all. But we won't tell The Fox. 80/20 split."

Kyle kicked a pebble on the ground, then nodded. "I hope to hell that I'm the 80 in that split."

"You are, man. Just taking a little cut to hold me over. Like a finder's fee. Plus, just think of it like you're buying my kids extra food at Carowinds."

Kyle laughed. "Yeah, that's exactly how I'll picture it then." He reached for the door. "Send me whatever I need to know. Are you usually running the same route or what?"

"Reedy Creek side. Pick up location varies, but I almost always drop by the bridge next to the lake. There's a box underneath the bridge you can access from the far side of the trail. Just duck under and toss it in the box. I'll text you the code and all that."

"Code?"

"Yeah, mine has a code that changes each time. Yours doesn't?" Andy whispered.

"Nah, man. It's just a log in the woods." Kyle whispered. "When I first started, I would run right past it because it blends in so well. Kind of genius if you ask me."

"I have nothing but reverence for The Fox." Andy mimicked a bow.

"Reverence? Who left a dictionary in the history teacher's lounge?"

Andy let out a guttural laugh and playfully shoved Kyle. "I owe you one, dude."

He let himself out of the room, and Kyle prepared for the day.

Once third period rolled around, Kyle found his mood had dramatically improved. As class shuffled in, he wrote the lesson topic on the board for the day and waited for somebody to raise their hand. Without fail, round-faced Harrison's hand sprung up from his side.

"Yes, Harrison?"

"Uh, Mr. P, you want to talk about monsters?"

"Yes. Would you like to start us off?"

"I know, like, the Pixar movie," Harrison said.

"That's Monsters, Inc., Dumbass!" A voice barked from the back row. Tommy Bruno's voice was unmistakable, but Kyle opted to skip the finger-pointing.

"Now, now. Let's settle down." Kyle paused and let the class simmer. "Why do I want to talk about monsters today?"

"Because of Frankenstein. He's, like, a monster," Kelsey added from the side of the class.

"Excellent. Now, can anybody describe the monster for me?" Kyle reached for a whiteboard marker. "I'll write adjectives you shout out up here on the board."

The voices came like a chorus. Within a minute, Kyle had written, "Angry" "Evil" "Huge" "Scary" and "Gross". He turned back to the class. "Alright, I need a volunteer."

Crickets.

"Let me rephrase. I need a volunteer to create a sentence about the monster using two of these adjectives or I'll fire at random."

Kelsey and the whole back row looked out the window. Kyle opted to turn back to the front row, where Megan Zahor eagerly waved her hand. He reluctantly pointed in her direction.

"Frankenstein is evil because he is huge and angry," Megan said and then flashed a smile.

"You did indeed fit two adjectives in that sentence." Kyle nodded at her and held up three fingers. "Three, actually. Excellent work on that part. But can somebody tell me what was incorrect about Megan's sentence?"

Megan deflated like a balloon under the word *incorrect*. Nobody raised their hand to dispute her. Megan looked like somebody just elected her Class President. Kyle turned to the side of the class. "Kelsey, what can you tell me about that sentence?"

"Uh, it was fine. Short but, like, not bad."

"And did you see anything incorrect about what Megan said? It's not her fault. This is a common mistake about the novel."

"I think she mixed up Frankenstein and the monster."

"Say more, Kelsey."

"Well, like Frankenstein is the scientist." Kelsey sat up straighter in her seat. "The monster is the monster. He name is not Frankenstein. So, if she said that the monster was evil and scary, that would be correct."

"Another excellent point." Kyle smiled. "I appreciate your input, Kelsey. Does everybody understand the excellent point that Kelsey has made?"

Murmurs of hums and head nods followed. A hand shot up in the front row. Harrison again. Kyle considered letting the boy off the hook in fear that he'd embarrass himself further, but wanted to honor his passion. "Harrison? What's up?"

"Well, I agree that the monster's name is not Frankenstein in the book." Harrison turned slightly red. "So, Kelsey is right about that. But I thought about it last night, and I think there may be two monsters in the book."

"Say more, Harrison," Kyle said with a grin. Usually, the honors classes failed to make such a clever distinction.

"Frankenstein is the monster too. He's the monster who made the monster. He's just as responsible for any destruction and death as the monster is. Maybe more responsible."

"Another excellent point. This has been a spirited discussion so far! It seems like you all are digging this story. Let's dive into Chapter Ten together. Okay?"

Kyle turned to open his pocket-sized copy of the book, and somebody whispered in the back of the class. "The only monster here is that zit on your nose, Harrison."

Kyle shot up from his chair and towered over Tommy Bruno's seat. "Mr. Bruno, do you have something to say to the entire class?"

Tommy suppressed a smile and shook his head with his best Eddie Haskell impression. "No, sir."

"Well, I think it's only fair that you let the Vice Principal know that you have some additional thoughts on the matter. Why don't you go check in with him and then come see me after class?"

"But—" Tommy fumbled for words.

"The only butts here is yours getting out of that chair and marching down to the office."

The entire class watched as Tommy Bruno stormed out in a fury and shouted a curse word in the hallway. "Anybody else with any thoughts?" Kyle asked to the class of mimes. The crickets were back.

"Great, Megan, lead us off with the first five paragraphs of Chapter Ten."

As Megan stuttered her way through the opening lines of the chapter, Kyle's mind was adrift. Floating in the ocean. Yet, somehow, even in a far off tropical land, Kyle heard Harrison's observation bouncing around his brain. Through all of the work, all of the jobs from The Fox, the lines had become blurred. It was hard to tell who the monster was these days.

CHAPTER ELEVEN

ZOE KEPT one eye on the clock while she worked. The second hand moved about as fast as one of Ernest's stories. She pulled her phone out of the drawer; a trick she used to keep herself from constantly checking for updates. *Nothing.* The clatter of the Visitor's Center door woke Zoe from her daze, and she looked up to see a bobbing wave of strawberry-red hair float her way.

She extended her arms for a hug. "Joanne! You're back!"

Joanne Mitchell grinned from ear to ear. "Did y'all miss me? I bet y'all missed me like squirrel missing a nut. Do I look tan?"

Zoe surveyed Joanne's tiny frame. "A bit, yeah! Where were you?"

"Just taking in the last of the sun down in Myrtle Beach."

"Did you have any company? Mr. Mysterious join you?"

Joanne blushed. "He came by for a weekend, but that's all you'll get out of me. I like to keep things quiet. I'm not one for all the attention that comes with that whole kiss and tell attitude." She looked into the back and then whispered, "Did they stick you at the desk the entire time?"

Zoe grinned. "Not the whole time, but most of it, as you predicted before you left."

"I'm sorry, dear. I assumed they'd stop this boy's club nonsense at some point."

"Well, maybe they will when you join the ranks. How's your application process going this time?"

Joanne's smile evaporated. "Rejected again. I know I'm not of a cookie-cutter background they like to hire around here, but I thought a few years on the job at this desk would take me further than it has." She let out a deep sigh.

"Come on now, you've got to keep at it. I'll continue to put in a good word when I can. That is when I'm not cursing your name for being the reason I'm shackled to a desk," Zoe said.

Joanne laughed and tossed her bag onto the desk. "Shackled? They can't cage a bird like you."

Zoe rolled her eyes and watched Joanne sort through her bag. The backpack was old and worn. A Jansport that likely had been her school bag decades ago. Patches clung to threads that attached them to the bag. One had her initials, JRM. Another had a small dog, fox, and a coyote. The biggest one was a patch of trees that resembled the forests within Umstead.

Joanne looked up. "Before I let you free, catch me up on the gossip?"

Zoe beamed. "With pleasure." She swapped spots with Joanne and let her take the chair. "Ernest still hasn't decided if this year will be his last, so Mathias was in a foul mood most of the week. I'm talking about an unkempt mustache Mathias. The real deal. Grumbling about the budget or something."

"I'm willing to bet that if Mathias took one of those fancy DNA tests, it'd tell him he was a direct descendent of Oscar the Grouch."

Zoe cracked up. "How long have you been saving that one?"

Joanne beamed. "Thought of it on the beach and wrote it down so I wouldn't forget. What about our resident southerner?"

"Clem said he caught the biggest bass he's ever seen down at

Crabtree Lake. He's got a photo of the catch set as his phone background, so if you so much as breathe near him, he'll show you the evidence."

"Nice to know some things never change. Seems like another boring old week in Umstead," Joanne said with a grin.

Zoe walked towards the bullpen. "Oh! And we had two more sightings."

Joanne rubbed her hands together in anticipation. "Saved the juicy bit for last, eh? What's going on?"

"Two more pins on the map. One by a pair of teenage boys, just south of the overpass on Big Lake. Another by a man fishing over on the other side of the park by Five-Turn Hill."

"Anybody have anything new to report or just the same old big scary ape in the woods bit?"

"Same as always. They either saw it from a distance or it ran from them. Usually, pre-dawn or nighttime if it's somebody in the campground."

"I swear, either we need to get some new eye doctors in Raleigh or there's something supernatural going on around here. Gee whiz."

"I've kept my doubts. It seems like some manufactured mayhem to me."

"And what do you believe is the root cause of this mayhem, Ranger Watts?" Joanne pretended to hold a pen up like a microphone for Zoe.

"Me?" Zoe shrugged. "Your guess is as good as mine. Gil on the other hand..."

"I'd imagine he's leading the charge into the wilderness to hunt for the hide of this thing."

"Don't get me started." Zoe laughed.

"Who would have guessed that the Bigfoot expert would be convinced that Bigfoot was visiting urban North Carolina?"

Zoe lowered her voice to a whisper. "He's been patient about it so far, but I think he crossed a line last night."

Joanne propped her head on her hands and her elbows on the table like a teen at a slumber party. "Go on."

"Somebody tipped off the authorities that there have been unusual sightings inside the park. Things that could be dangerous to the public."

"Could've been one of those kids, no?"

"Could be, but I doubt it," Zoe said. "The way Mathias talked about it, it sure sounded like somebody put together a compelling argument to make us take action."

Joanne grinned. "And what action did our fearless leader choose?"

"Informational posters and game cameras in areas of frequent sightings."

"So, the usual spots? Off Big Lake's social trail and where Sycamore crosses the bike and bridle trail?"

Zoe smiled. "And somebody said you weren't ready to be a park ranger? Please."

"Need to get you on the hiring committee." Joanne blushed. "Well, go off. Make yourself scarce. Don't stick around the indoors on my account. Go be the wild woman that you are."

"I'll be off the next few days, by the way," Zoe added from the hallway.

"Pre-wedding honeymoon for you and Gil? I can give you the name of the place where I was in Myrtle."

"I wish, but this is just as good. My cousin Delaney is coming to town. Best person in the world. Like a sister to me. She lives up north in Massachusetts, so I don't see her as much as I'd like. Nowadays just holidays and reunions."

Joanne stacked some papers on her desk. "Well, if anybody deserves a break, it's you. Drink an extra marg for me, dear," she said with a grin.

Zoe nodded and gathered her things from her desk in the back. She caught the clock as it struck four and sprinted out the door. She sped towards home and made the twelve-mile drive in under ten minutes. When she pulled up, Gil was sitting on the front porch.

"Have you heard from Delaney?" he asked as he approached Zoe's truck.

"They said sometime around four was their ETA. Should be any minute."

"That is a sixty-watt smile you have brought home with you today. Did somebody get off desk duty or is this just pure unbridled cousin-infused excitement?"

"Both, actually. But despite my sunny disposition, I need to talk with you."

"The words that every man dreads. Go on."

The sound of an approaching vehicle distracted them both. A car slowed to a crawl down the access road. Hikers and cyclists whirred past in a blur. Zoe waved her entire body like an inflatable outside of a used car lot. As the car neared, she could see Delaney inside, fumbling with her seat belt.

She turned to Gil and put a hand on his shoulder. "Saved by the bell, Gilbert."

Gil faked wiping sweat from his brow and started towards the driveway. Zoe followed and whispered in the split-second before the car doors opened. "I know you tipped them off," she said. Gil turned white as a ghost.

CHAPTER TWELVE

THE ROAD NARROWED as they turned off the highway and approached a maroon gate between two brick columns and a sign that said 'William B. Umstead State Park'. Shadows from the loblolly pines above danced on the concrete near the entrance. Hoagie sniffed at the air wafting in through the open window.

"Here we are!" Delaney said, not even attempting to hide her glee.

"That wasn't so bad. You sick of me yet?" Casper asked.

"You've passed the test for the first twelve hours. Prepare for your next challenge. Cousin Zoe awaits," Delaney said.

"I hope this is more Super Mario than Mortal Kombat," Casper said as he looked out at the surrounding forest. "This park is so lush. The pine trees are fragrant. Smells like a candle that my mom would have lit around Christmas time."

He lowered his window and took in the fresh as daisies evening air. October in Massachusetts was more winter than fall, but North Carolina clung to every bit of summer, somehow two seasons behind the northern states.

"I love it here. I've only been here once when Zoe first moved

66

in a few years back. Since then, she's come up to see me or met our families in Jersey."

"Another pine forest to explore, Hoagie."

"Let's try to stay out of trouble this time, boys," Delaney said.

Delaney slowed the car to a crawl and turned right past an *Authorized Personnel Only* sign. "For the time being, we're authorized personnel. Just don't tell Zoe's boss."

They passed a crosswalk where a narrow trail traversed the pavement and carried on to their right into a thicket of rhododendrons and laurels. The path looked narrow, a single-track that was blanketed with pine needles. The terrain reminded Casper of Cape Cod and The Punkhorns. The road ended and a small house sat to their left next to two old shabby sheds labeled *Maintenance* that dotted the dead end.

The house had brown siding that was weathered and worn. A small covered garden bed sat raised above the grass to the right of the copper-colored shed that butted up against the forest on the back of the property. A gravel driveway held three vehicles, one of which was a dented and rusty-patched truck that said RANGER on the side. The overgrown lawn was more crabgrass than grass. Small puddles of water sat stagnant on the far side of the lot.

Before Casper could say a word, Zoe rushed out the door and sprinted towards Delaney with her arms spread wide. They both squealed, and the sound pierced Casper's eardrums.

At first glance, Zoe looked nothing like Delaney. Her short-cropped blonde hair stood in stark contrast to Delaney's black-coffee, shoulder-length cut. There didn't appear to be a single freckle on Zoe's face, but instead, she carried an even tan from all of her work in the sunshine. She had the same build as Delaney, fit and strong with an appearance that all but assured that she could kick any man's ass. Meeting his stare, Zoe broke the embrace and jogged around the front hood of the car toward Casper.

"And you must be the infamous Casper Kelly," she said with an extended hand.

Casper smiled. "And you must be the legendary Zoe Watts. What a pleasure!"

He brushed aside the extended hand and embraced Zoe with a hug. As he looked over her shoulder, Delaney gave him a wink.

"You've passed your first test, Casper Kelly. But I fear that you had some serious tutoring in the car from Laney about my disdain for handshakes amongst family."

"I plead the fifth," Casper said.

A man with copper-brown wavy hair and wire-frame glasses stood on the front steps and watched the embrace. He had big wide eyes like a barn owl that made his tiny mouth look even smaller than it truly was. His mop of hair fell in stray strands across his forehead and over his ears. He grinned at the visitors and sauntered over without a word. Delaney gave him a big hug and then turned to introduce Casper.

"Casper, this is Gil. Gil, Casper."

"Pleasure. Welcome to Umstead." Gil's smile was warm, but his eyes looked like those of a man who had just escaped a turbulent plane ride. "May I help with your bags?"

"Gladly. But first let me release the beast. I hope you guys like dogs because Hoagie will demand your full attention," Casper said as he gripped the door handle.

He pulled and Hoagie shot out like a cannonball. He darted around from person to person, rolling onto his back and waiting for a belly rub. Zoe smiled widely, leaned down, and scratched, wide-eyed. "Oh, Hoagie. You're too cute."

After a raucous dinner of homemade shrimp tacos and two rounds of lime margaritas, the foursome sprawled across the living room. Hoagie curled up next to Zoe, who scratched at his chin. Without a second of silence, Zoe asked Casper to recount the harrowing tale of the case that had brought Delaney into his life. He did his best to make it sound compelling. She hung on every word. After the ending, she kept shaking her head and saying "wow" to herself over and over.

Zoe stepped into the kitchen to help Gil put another round of margaritas in the blender and Casper turned to Delaney. "You were right."

"I know. But about what?"

"Zoe is a firecracker," Casper whispered.

"She's a hoot. I'm glad y'all are getting along."

"Did you just say y'all?"

Delaney shushed him with a kiss.

Casper tried to shift attention away from his casework and onto the true mystery in the room: Gil. He sat cross-legged on the recliner chair staring intently at whoever was speaking.

"So, Gil. We listened to a bit of your podcast on the way down. Great stuff. Gripping."

Gil's eyes lit up. "Ah, so you were the one!" Gil laughed. "Thank you for that review. At which episode did you stop?"

"How many was it, Delaney? I think we were around the time you explained the history of sightings on the east coast."

"That is towards the end! Color me impressed. Even my mother could not suffer through that much of it."

"So much research!" Delaney said with an eye towards Zoe.

"Ah, on the shoulders of giants. There is great research out there. However, I was able to tap into some of my own for the east coast analysis. There is actually a town close to here that believes they are the home of the one and only Bigfoot."

"And is that true?" Delaney asked.

"I'd say it is likely to be a hoax. Or a flawed belief at the core," Gil said. "However, they have built an industry on it, much like the Pacific Northwest. I am not here to disrupt the local economy. On your return voyage, you will drive past it. Littleton, North Carolina. Sixty-three miles north. Next to the Virginia border. They have a Cryptozoology museum that is scientifically questionable but a quite humorous trip!"

"Crypto-what?" Delaney said.

"Cryptozoology. It's the study of animals whose existence is unsubstantiated to date," Casper added.

Gil pointed towards Casper. "I now understand cousin Delaney's admiration for you, Casper Kelly! I must ask, I read up on your career. Have you run into anything similar on any of your cases?"

Casper laughed. "Not yet. My cases often center around something deemed unexplainable. Something that makes little sense to the naked eye or feels like it's supernatural."

"Elaborate," Gil said with wide eyes.

"Sometimes. It's a whole mix of things, but without fail, there is always an explanation. People hire me when they need answers to questions nagging at them or causing danger to fall upon an area. But often, there's a human element behind it all."

Zoe craned her neck and looked into the driveway. "Funny, I didn't see the Mystery Machine when you pulled up."

Gil pressed on anyway. "Well, time for the million-dollar question Casper. Do you believe in Bigfoot?"

Zoe rolled her eyes and sipped her drink. Casper chuckled and looked to Delaney for help, but she averted her eyes. He was on his own. "I'm inclined to believe something until proven otherwise. But I look forward to reading your book to help firm up my stance."

Delaney gave him a subtle nod, as if to tell him he handled that well. Gil cracked a smile and then darted out of the room. Zoe shook her head. Hoagie let out a yelp of displeasure at being woken from his dream by all the hubbub.

"Where's he going?" Delaney asked.

"I never know what he's up to, Laney. Most times, that's for the best."

"Laney. Now that's something I'd like to talk about. What other embarrassing details can you share with me about our lovely Laney here?" Casper asked.

Gil shuffled back into the room with a large corkboard that had a map on it. Pins dotted the trails that spidered through the map. Casper watched Gil set it up on the coffee table and hold it up for all to see. "Maybe this will help firm up your stance in the meantime," Gil said with a grin.

Zoe slumped in her chair and put her head in her hands. "Jesus, no, Gil. They just got here."

He continued as if he didn't hear her. "In the last six months, there have been twelve Bigfoot sightings here inside Umstead State Park!"

Gil let the words hang around in the air for a full minute. He led Casper and Delaney through the recent rash of sightings while Zoe watched her ice cubes melt.

Delaney broke out into a fit of laughter. Casper looked around in confusion. He turned to Zoe. "Is this... real?"

She shrugged. "Yes, and no. We've had reports of weird stuff. Not everybody has used the term Bigfoot but we're seeing things that—What was that you said earlier, Casper? Things that seem unexplainable."

"Could it be a bear or—" Delaney asked.

Zoe scoffed. "It could literally be anything. I'd like to look into it, but just to prove this idiot here wrong. He thinks it's Bigfoot. Most folks think it's probably just kids pulling a prank."

"But Bigfoot... in North Carolina?" Casper said.

Gil smiled. "There are local urban legends in communities across the country and around the world. I'm sure you've heard the word Yeti or Sasquatch thrown around, yes?"

Casper nodded. "But that's not a Bigfoot?"

Gil grinned. "Until somebody catches one, we won't know for certain, but there's a variety of large creatures roaming around different parts of the United States."

"Like what? I'd like to know what to keep an eye out for while we hike tomorrow," Delaney said.

"In Florida, there are stories of a Skunk Ape. Similar to Bigfoot, it's a big primate that people see occasionally. In Arkansas, they tell stories about the Ozark Howler. In Puerto Rico, they all fear the Chupacabra. New Orleans has the Rougarou."

"The what?"

"Basically, a large werewolf."

Zoe groaned, which made Delaney cackle.

"Okay, but is there proof of any of this?" Casper asked.

Gil tapped on the map. "What is that adage? Seeing is believing or believing is seeing? Most experts would argue that we see what we believe in and dismiss the rest."

"But imagine you had to sell it to a skeptic like me..."

"Are you religious, Casper?" Gil steepled his hands. "I do not mean to intrude, but I hope you will indulge me."

Casper shook his head. "I tend to agree with Pascal's Wager. I'd rather live my life as if there is a God and find out there isn't than..."

"So, why is your belief template so different for cryptids? Would it not be simpler or more prudent to live as if they are real and find out they are not?"

Zoe let out a groan and put her head in her hands.

"Because these... things you named are absurd and unproven," Delaney said.

"If somebody believes in God, they see signs all around them to confirm that belief. If they do not believe, they interpret signs around them as further proof that God does not exist. I do not mean to lump God and Bigfoot into the same sentence, but I hope you follow."

"So, like, confirmation bias?"

Gil nodded. "If you are a Bigfoot believer, you look at the evidence, sightings, reports, and footprints as confirmation. If you are an unbeliever, you see it as madness and dismiss it outright."

"I follow," Casper said. He flopped backward onto the couch. "Gil, if your book is half as compelling as your argument here, it'll be a best seller."

"That would require a completed manuscript, which feels about evasive as Bigfoot at the moment." Gil smiled.

Delany eyed the room and then let out a chuckle. "Some vacation, huh?"

Zoe jumped to her feet. "Ding ding ding. Did you hear that bell, Gil? That's the alert when you've hit your Bigfoot limit for the evening. We have guests. Let's catch up and get drunk. Is that too much to ask?" she said.

Delaney raised her glass, and the others followed. "To family!"

Casper put his glass in the air and smiled. "To catching Bigfoot!"

CHAPTER THIRTEEN

"This is 713, we've got a code red down by Reedy Creek Lake. Uh, 10-33. 10-33." The radio static woke Zoe from a fitful sleep. Gil let out a groan but turned over to his side and put his pillow over his ear to muffle the sound from the speaker. It blared again. Clem's voice. "This is 713, we've got a code red down by Reedy Creek Lake. 10-33."

Zoe shot out of bed, sprinted to her closet, and threw on half of her uniform. Her house was the closest to the location Clem had shouted through the radio. This was her chance.

One Mississippi. They drilled the code system into Zoe's brain from her first day on the job. Certain codes echoed through the radios daily. A 10-7 meant somebody was offline for lunch.

Five Mississippi. 10-53 meant an illegally parked car in the lot. 10-45 was roadkill. Plenty more mundane number combinations that solicited little more than a yawn from park staff. But 10-33? 10-33 meant drop everything and get there now. Somebody was in danger.

Nine Mississippi. Without tying her boots, Zoe sprinted toward the maintenance shed that sat two hundred yards away. Her hands

74

shook so badly that she could barely locate the key to the shed on the overcrowded ring that typically hung from her belt and accumulated dust. She pulled off the lock and threw it to the side.

Twelve Mississippi. A tug on the garage door cord lifted it open. Within seconds, Zoe had kicked the ATV into gear and sped out of the lot and down the hill towards Clem's location.

Fifteen Mississippi. Loblolly pines stood like a shocked audience as she tore down the path. She tried to think of a reason that Clem would need help at such a peculiar hour. Plus, Clem was off today. That didn't add up.

Twenty Mississippi. Either way, there was no reasonable excuse why Clem would be on this side of the park at this ungodly hour and in need of emergency assistance.

Twenty-five Mississippi. The radio crackled, and she tucked her head into her shoulder to listen. Clem had called for EMTs. This was serious. From the initial information Zoe had, she assumed Clem was not the one injured. A rough-and-tumble man like Clem Jenkins would be hard-pressed to call in such a panic if he'd just rolled his ankle or taken a fall. No, somebody else was hurt. Seriously hurt.

Thirty Mississippi... As she crested the hill, she could see Clem down on the ground, kneeling next to the body. He stood and waved her over. She threw the vehicle into park and hopped off, sprinting towards Clem and the body next to him.

"Is he breathing?"

"Barely," Clem whispered.

"Pulse?"

"I checked when I first arrived. It was low, but it was present." Zoe knelt and placed two fingers on his neck. A faint pulse throbbed beneath her fingertips.

She dove into her bag and tossed the first aid kid out in front of her. She looked over the body. The man was middle-aged. Fit. Scratches and blood covered his shirt. His eyes were open, watching her as she looked him over.

"We're going to get you some help, okay? I just need to find the source of all this blood."

The man gave a slight nod and slumped his head back onto the trail. Zoe turned to Clem. "Can you get gauze and bandages out of that bag? Antiseptic too."

Clem did as instructed and handed Zoe each item. Zoe paused for a second and then tore the open man's shirt. Her stomach lurched. Remnants of margaritas and shrimp came firing into her esophagus. She gulped it down. "This looks like-" She shook her head and squinted at the wounds. "Hell, I don't know."

"Same." Clem tugged at his shirt. "What do we do? You're born for this shit."

"Me?"

"Yeah, don't bullshit me. What's the procedure?" Clem stared into the injured man's wounds. "Is... is that fur?"

Zoe met his eyes and tried to ignore the question. "Not relevant. Once we stop the bleeding, we need to get him off the trail and somewhere that the ambulance can pick him up. I have the flat board on the back of the ATV. We can attach him and transport him out. Where will the EMTs go?"

"Up by the entrance gate, off Harrison. They've got a code for the gate in situations like this, but I doubt they know it. They may cut the lock but it depends on the crew."

Zoe nodded and did her best to treat the deepest wounds. She looked the man in the eyes and spoke softly to him. "We're going to get you to the hospital, okay?"

His eyes blinked but he didn't say anything. Zoe knew the tell-tale signs of shock from training. "Remember to breathe. This may hurt as we lift you, okay?"

After a second, she turned to Clem. "Alright, help me get him onto the flat board safely and then I'll head up to meet the ambulance." Zoe removed the yellow stretcher-board from the back of the ATV and laid it next to the man's body. "Remember how this works?"

Clem nodded, and they shifted the man carefully onto the stretcher, carried it over to the ATV, and hooked it onto the back portion. Tight. No wiggle room.

Zoe hopped onto the vehicle and turned the ignition. The engine roared again. Clem stared at his bloody hands and looked up at her.

"What should I do?" he asked.

Zoe thought he looked scared. As white as a ghost. "You wait here. Check the perimeter for anything suspicious."

"But what if it-"

"Clem, we have a man clinging to life back here." She handed him her pistol. "Stand guard. If you see something coming at you, shoot it."

Clem nodded. "Zoe?"

Zoe strapped her helmet tight and shot him a look.

Clem's voice was low, barely audible. "I'm... I'm sorry I didn't believe you. You know, about the..."

Zoe nodded and kicked the ATV into a higher gear. She sped up and out of the valley and back toward the parking lot. Halfway back, she saw Mathias' truck approach, but she pressed the gas toward the floor and sped towards the gate. *You're not dying on my watch, bud.* Mathias veered onto the shoulder of the road and whipped his truck around. His headlights lit the path in front of Zoe better than the shoddy bulbs of the ATV that shook from her speed. The glow of red siren lights in the distance told her to turn left at the intersection. Like Clem had guessed, the EMTs were stuck at the gate without their access code.

The EMTs swarmed the ATV like bees toward a flower, and she stepped out of the way. A young wide-eyed man stood with a pair of bolt cutters at his side, jaw dropped the bloody mess Zoe had hauled up from the trail.

Zoe gave them space. They were the experts here. She was just a cog in the well-oiled machine of emergency response. Mathias walked over toward her and nodded his head.

"Thank you," he said. "I'm glad it was you on top of this. You handled this well. It's no longer a secret that you're overqualified for your job here."

"Just doing my part, sir," Zoe responded. Her eyes remained locked on the man's body as they raised him into the back of the ambulance and sped off. A flood of police cars approached and crowded the area around the gate.

"Mind if I steal your wheels?" Mathias asked. "I'd like to go check on Clem."

Zoe nodded and handed him the keys. The newly arrived police approached as Ernest pulled up and parked behind them. Mathias sped off and Zoe braced herself for a sea of questions about the most hectic five minutes of her life. One of the EMTs stayed behind. They spoke with a tall woman who appeared to be in charge. She moved with authority. Tall and upright, like a rooster strutting. She had long black hair and tan skin. A smile never left her face as she stepped towards Zoe.

"Ranger Watts?" She extended a hand as she spoke. "I'm Detective Chandler Russo. I hear you were first on the scene?" Russo spoke with the faint hint of a New Jersey accent.

Zoe shook her hand and nodded. "Second. I answered the call from my colleague, Clem Jenkins. He may have the answers you're looking for, Detective."

Russo shook her head. "No need for formalities. We're colleagues here. Both women of the law. You can just call me Chandler."

Zoe nodded. "Did the EMTs have any updates for you? First impressions?"

Russo shook her head again. "Nothing concrete, but there is reason for optimism. Still, it may be a long road ahead." She pulled out a notepad and clicked a pen. "Can you recount what you saw?"

"What I saw?"

"Essentially, I need to decide if this was an assault or a freak accident."

"I'm no expert, but—"

"Gut instincts. It's like when you see an asshole walk into a bar. You know what you're looking at before he opens his mouth. What is your body telling you?"

"Nothing I saw made me think this was an accident," Zoe said.

"Well then, we're on the same page already. Will you look at that? While we're at it, mind walking me through the rest of it? Your approach and anything else you think would be helpful?"

Zoe recounted the call and the subsequent moments down by the lake with Clem. The detective nodded along, clearly well-versed in the art of active listening with her *mhm's* and *okay's*. Zoe left out the part about the fur in the wounds and the recent peculiar activities within the park boundaries.

"Well, I can say without a doubt that we're all lucky that you were there so quickly. It seems your co-worker was in over his head, so to speak." Russo sighed. "Not everybody can handle the grittier parts of the job."

Zoe forced a smile and heard the roar of an approaching ATV. In the distance, she saw that Clem had saddled up onto the ATV with Mathias. Every pair of eyes at the gate turned and watched. Zoe let out an exhale as the spotlight shifted away.

Russo nodded towards the oncoming vehicle and turned to Zoe. "Here's my card. Cell is on the back. If anything comes up, I'll update you. And thank you again." They shook hands again. "There's a damn good chance that Wade Buchanon is likely alive because of you."

"Wade who?"

"That was the victim's name. EMTs found a medical bracelet on his wrist. Some runners wear them in case of an accident. Much like his today, although..."

Zoe nodded. "Thank you. It's nice to know his name at least."

Russo put a gentle hand on Zoe's shoulder, smiled, and turned to Mathias and Clem. Zoe skirted away from the scene. She wandered towards home, letting the celebrity of Clem's arrival serve as a necessary distraction so that she could exit peacefully. The serene stroll through the early morning sounds of nature was a welcome distraction as she approached her cottage. Spike balls from sweet gum trees dotted the path like an abstract painting.

All the while, Zoe flashed back to the man she'd seen under the bloody mess. Wade Buchanon. The man who went for a jog and ran into trouble. She ached for his family, who were likely anxiously awaiting his return, sitting around the breakfast table listening for the sound of his car in their driveway. She whispered a silent prayer to no one that he someday return to them in peace.

Every shadow that lurked between the trees startled her more than usual. Every crunch of leaves grew louder. She shook it off, focused on the birds instead. But soon, the sound was unmistakable. Before and after park hours, the only folks that were supposed to be in the park were staff and family. Usually, the sound of approaching footsteps was no cause for concern. But after Zoe's hellish morning, she was on guard and prepared for the worst.

CHAPTER FOURTEEN

THE WIND CUT like a knife as the car swung down on the tracks and careened towards certain death. Everybody around Andy screamed in fear. Manufactured agony. *Why in the world do people do this to themselves?* He laughed it off.

His son, Andrew, clawed at Andy's arm, nails dug in with a fierceness that would soon leave a mark. Andy smiled at him and tried his best to feign reassurance. It was impossible to communicate over the roar of the coaster and there were no words that Andy could string together that would calm Andrew down.

Ava, the older of the two, sat unenthused by the ride. Andy had no doubt that she'd rather be scrolling through her phone than riding a rickety roller coaster with her old man. It didn't hurt that she reminded him of that preference at least four times on the two-hour-drive south. Andy understood. All he wanted was to chain smoke cigarettes while he anxiously checked his phone. Instead, his legs wailed in agony under the too-tight seatbelt of a decades-old roller coaster that was careening through its final turns.

Once the ride slowed to a halt, Andy turned to Ava. "Fun, right?"

She rolled her eyes. "Can we go now? I have band practice tonight."

"No way! Dad promised us at least four roller coasters!" Andrew shouted with glee. "That means two more. Minimum!"

Such a big word out of such a tiny mouth made Andy chuckle. "Can't break a promise to the kid, you know." Andy nudged Ava with his shoulder. "Come on, A. I'll buy you a soda before the next one."

"Ew, soda is gross," she snorted.

"You used to love soda." He scratched at his head. "Root beer, right? I can't keep up with things these days. Your preferences change as often as traffic lights. Or maybe I'm just getting old."

"You are old, Dad. But it's okay," Andrew said with a smile. Ava let out a quiet giggle.

As they waited in line for the next coaster, one that promised a screaming good time, Andy thought of Kyle. How he had faired with the job. He didn't have the nerve to check his bank account yet, but knew that The Fox was prompt. If the money wasn't in his account within the next twenty minutes, something was wrong.

Not that Andy expected something to go wrong. Much the opposite. Things had gone smoothly for so long that there were no signs of trouble. The waters were calm. Smooth sailing. Andy was grateful that Kyle roped him into the gig and owed him a debt of gratitude for the lifeline. And now a debt of 80% of this morning's job. Assuming the job went off without a hitch.

He felt certain that someday soon, his ex-wife would wake up to find his face on the news in connection with a string of drug arrests. He'd lose his kids forever and probably his job too. Every crime show he watched on Netflix reassured him that the low-level players get caught and flipped for information. They're just chum that's flipped around to bring in a bigger fish. Or a bigger fox, in this case. With each passing week and new set of instructions from The Fox, he'd kick himself for not being smarter when he was younger. For gambling away his savings. His 401k. And then Regina's. But a light shone at the end of his metaphorical tunnel, although the terrain within the tunnel was murky and riddled with challenges.

When Ava hurried in to use the bathroom, Andy glanced at his phone and saw no message from Kyle. There was, however, an alert from his bank. The deposit was pending in his account. Andy let himself smile and exhale a breath he'd been holding in since yesterday. Still, the lack of communication from Kyle nagged at his brain. *Probably waltzing through the forest waiting for his payday.*

Fire roared in his lungs. His quads screamed in agony as he tore through the brush. Pain pushed through to his hamstrings and calves. He leaped over a downed log and dodged dead trees that were like slaloms on the downward slope. Every obstacle that nature had came for him with full force.

The fallen leaves on the forest floor were loose and Kyle lost his footing. Again and again. Tumbling like a toddler practicing gymnastics. Each time he fell and felt his body collide with the ground, he flung himself forward and picked up his pace once again. After ten minutes and what felt like ten miles, he took his first glance backward. Nothing. Nobody was in sight. The sirens that once filled the air had died down, and there was no pitter-patter of footsteps in pursuit of him. He had escaped. For now.

He slowed to a jog and ditched the long-sleeve black shirt, hoping to create a disguise. Near the base of an oak, he dropped the shirt, covered it with soil, and kicked some leaves on top. Anybody that would have seen him would look for a man in a long-sleeve black Nike running shirt with forest green shorts and a gray cap. The cap dug into his hip from its spot in his waistband. The autumn sun continued its ascent as the warmth of the day helped soothe the goosebumps on his chilly arms.

The smell of pine trees seemed toxic, reminiscent of copper in Kyle's nose. He could only smell blood. His eyes flashed images of the man's body on the trail. The blood was so dark. It was nothing like the movies. Red wasn't the right color. Crimson was too light. Midnight sky dark. More black than red. It was unlike anything he'd ever seen. Authors had gone to great lengths to describe the liquid that pumps through a human's veins and keeps us alive. But Kyle had never seen it in that quantity. In such a horrific display.

He tried to shake the thought from his mind and instead pictured Andy. He would still get his cut. Somewhere, he was loading his kids into the backseat of his Honda Civic and cruising just above the speed limit towards Carowinds. The breeze would blow through their youthful faces as they rode the ups and downs of the roller coasters. Andy would overpay for cotton candy and pizza for lunch. He'd sneak them extra sweets to win them over and curry some favor away from his ex-wife. The thoughts were soothing. Like an alternate reality where Kyle was the loving divorced father of two and Andy was the criminal on the run. Literally, on the run.

Every fiber in Kyle's body rejected the daydream. He glanced backward again. Still nothing. His leg thumped against something stone. Upright. Rigid. From the ground, he looked up to see that he'd stumbled into a graveyard. In the middle of the forest, far off any nearby trail or sign of civilization, sat a collection of three small gravestones. Each worn and weathered. Words that were once carved had faded. There were no names, numbers, or any identifying information. Kyle looked to the sky.

"Okay, God. I get it. Message received. Loud and clear."

He let out a half-sob and trudged out of the clearing. The next mile dragged on like a marathon, but he made the march. He faced the stark reality of the moment as he took a cautious step out of the woods and onto the paved road that led to the entrance gate of the park. Morning joggers and bikers had parked their cars neatly in rows. Respectfully disrespecting the posted hours on the gate before them. Kyle tried to discern which of the cars belonged to the man. The now bloody, injured man who did not look like he would drive out of the park today.

At that moment, Kyle decided he was out. He had no choice but to wash his hands of everything. Find a clean slate. This part of his life was over. It was only a matter of time until he had a headstone of his own. No, that wasn't happening. He'd go home, empty his savings account and sever all ties. He was on to new things. New, sandy, salt-water soaked things. Things that didn't include the police or bloody crime scenes. Things that were within the boundaries of the law. This was the end.

CHAPTER FIFTEEN

THE MORNING SUN showered through the dense canopy of oak trees speckling the trail below. Casper stretched his arms wide and waited for Delaney to join him in the front yard. They'd both woken up from the sound of Zoe rushing out in the pre-dawn hours and been unable to fall back asleep. Delaney had suggested a walk on the trails before they huddled over steaming coffee cups and planned the rest of their route south.

"So, what do you think of everyone?" Delaney asked as she strolled out of the front door. Hoagie ambled down the steps and stretched out on the lawn.

"They're what I expected. Zoe is a blast. I can only imagine the trouble you two got into together as kids."

"I plead the fifth."

"Gil's not as bizarre as I'd expected when we heard that podcast. He's almost normal, but I can see the scientist in him. One of those kinds of people that use big words to describe little things. Like something out of a David Foster Wallace novel."

"He's grown on me over time, but I think I've just been happy to see Zoe happy. She'd had a lot of struggles before they met and somehow together they righted the ship."

"The park is spectacular; I'll say that much. I can't get over how close we are to Raleigh and yet it feels like we're deep inside Middle Earth or something."

Hoagie pawed at the dirt, trying to play with a bee that hovered above the ground. "Elf movie references aside, yeah, it's something else. Let's hit the trail and see some more of it."

Delaney led Casper down the road they'd driven in on and promised to navigate towards a footpath that led into the forest. "You get any sleep? You were tossing and turning a lot."

Casper shook his head. "New places. New bed. My pillow was lumpy. Nothing major."

"You sure?"

He nodded and swallowed his next prepared lie, embarrassed that Delaney noticed his restlessness. His mind spiraled through worst-case-scenarios of what Delaney could be hiding. A secret lovechild? A dangerous past? A criminal record? The thoughts came racing back with each step they took. Casper summoned the courage to speak.

"Can I ask you something?"

"Anything. What's up?"

Hoagie barked and Casper's eyes shifted toward a figure that approached in the distance. After careful steps forward, they breathed easy. It was Zoe. She had blood on her uniform and stared up at the clouds in the grayish-blue sky.

"Zo?" Delaney asked into the sunlight.

"Laney? Why in the world are you two lovebirds up at this hour?"

"Couldn't sleep. Heard the commotion this morning. What's up? Is that blood?"

"Unfortunately, yes. We had an assault on the trail this morning. One of the other rangers was first on the scene, but I was there shortly after. Ugly stuff," Zoe said.

"What's the status of the vic?" Delaney said.

Zoe laughed. "Can't take the cop out of you even when you're on vacation. He was a middle-aged man out on a jog. He was clinging to life when I got there, but he's at the hospital now. Hoping for the best."

"Shit, I'm so sorry. That's a hell of a way to start your day off," Delaney said. Hoagie looked up from the ground impatiently waiting for his overdue belly rub.

"Yeah, about that. There's a chance I'll need to head in to get in front of all of this. On the rare occasion somebody sprains an ankle on a trail, the whole town freaks out. I don't want to even consider how they'd react to news like this."

"Do whatever you need to do. We've got no agenda."

"Yeah, about that. Casper, remember your speech last night about the unexplainable? About your cases?"

"I wouldn't call it a speech but—"

Zoe stopped him. "Didn't mean that in a bad way. Just got me thinking."

"What's up?"

"There's already chatter within my team of rangers that this has something to do with those unusual sightings that Gil mentioned last night. Nobody is throwing the name Bigfoot around, but there's some discomfort with the timing of it all."

"Timing as in peculiar sightings recently, and now there's a violent crime for the first time in forever here?"

Zoe glanced at Delaney. "You're right. He's a quick learner. That's dead-on, Casper."

"And you're thinking that maybe this thing, er, *creature* is responsible?"

"I saw the wounds close up. They looked human, but..." Her voice trailed off.

"But what?" Delaney said.

"There was fur. Not a lot but some. It got my coworker Clem thinking, and he's the biggest skeptic of us all."

"That's rather unusual. Look, I'm happy to help but don't want to rub anybody the wrong way either," Casper said. He noticed Delaney nod at him. He picked up the cue. "But I think I could be a big help to the case if you'd be interested."

Delaney smiled wider than a billboard. Casper sighed from relief.

Zoe smiled too, but it was half-hearted and showcased her exhaustion from the morning's events. "Let me run it by Mathias and see what I can do. Money is likely to be an issue but—"

"Not necessary. I'm always happy to help family."

Zoe nodded. "Family. You're a sappy one at heart, aren't you, Casper?"

Casper grinned. "Guilty as charged. Just let me know. In the meantime, *Laney* here and I are going to head into the trails."

"Unless you want us to stick around and keep you company at home?" Delaney said.

"No, no. Please go. Gil will want to tend to me, and I need a shower before I head into the office. I'll catch up with you soon."

They nodded and Zoe walked past, strolling towards her cottage with her eyes fixed once again on the sky. Clouds were forming above them but the sun continued to shine through them, filtering the harsh rays and providing the perfect fall weather.

Hoagie led them off the main road and onto the trail. Roots sprung up from the ground and dove back into the soil a few feet away. The path was firm under Casper's feet and flat as a board. Nothing like the ankle-bending trails of The Punkhorns. Loose soil kicked up as they hiked deeper into the trees, weaving around towering pines and past small wooden benches that marked ideal spots for a scenic view. Hoagie didn't seem to mind. They wound down a switchback and then hitched up their step to climb the small hill nestled over a culvert that let out into a stream.

"She's a lot like you, you know?" Casper said as they crossed a footbridge that passed over a lazy creek.

"I've heard that before, but it's been years. What makes you say that?"

Casper dug for the right words. "You two are fierce."

"Fierce? You know how to talk to the ladies, Casper," Delaney laughed.

"Oh, I'm well aware. Just ask all two of my previous girlfriends."

"Is that a trap where you wait for me to tell you how many exes I have?"

"Not at all," Casper protested. "I was trying to be self-deprecating but—"

"Well, please give me their names and numbers. Maybe a list of their biggest fears and insecurities, too. I've got some Facebook messages to write when we get home."

"What did you think about what Zoe said? About the case?"

"She's got solid instincts, so it's weird to see her so rattled about something like this. I don't know what to make of it, but then again, the only evidence I have is the first half of Gil's unsolicited presentation last night."

"He sure is a character. But I find him charming somehow."

"I thought maybe you'd find him a kindred spirit. Not that you're a crypto-whatever person, but he's somebody not quite built for the nine-to-five life. A free spirit."

"If Zoe says she wants my help, would you join me?"

"You couldn't get rid of me if you tried, bud."

"I knew I liked you for a reason," Casper joked.

"Didn't you want to ask me something?"

Casper sighed. "It can wait." *Why ruin something so perfect? Nobody wants to clean up shattered glass.*

CHAPTER SIXTEEN

THE USUAL HUM of foot traffic through the automatic doors of the Visitor's Center had slowed to a buzz as the news of the assault spread around Raleigh. Runners and hikers that explored Umstead's trails daily were scarce, like a rainstorm was approaching. The park's emptiness left Zoe with a creepy feeling inside as she stared out the window into the empty parking lot.

The noise of a throat being cleared broke her stare, and she turned to find Clem Jenkins leaning against the window to her right.

"Zoe."

"Clem, how are you? I thought Mathias told you to take the day off."

"I'm alright. The EMTs looked me over and said that the shock would wear off after a few hours, but told me to take it easy. I'm avoiding heavy machinery, but I didn't want to miss this meeting."

"Any word from the hospital?"

"Mathias was on the phone with that detective lady earlier."

"Russo?"

"That's the one. She's the lead on the case. The latest bottleneck as we fight for information about what the hell happened."

"I'm glad you're doing okay, I—"

"I don't remember much from our conversation while you were saving my ass down by the lake, but I wanted to be sure that something was clear. I owe you many, many thanks."

"Just doing my job, Clem."

"You do it well and for the endless amounts of crap that we give you about being a woman or whatever, you've been an all-star from the start. You'll be running this place soon."

"If today's event is any indication, there won't be much to run. This place will be a ghost town unless we can piece together some answers."

"I hear you. But still—"

"Thank you, Clem. I appreciate your confidence in me. Sincerely."

Clem nodded and the shuffling of chair legs on the linoleum floor signaled the start of the staff meeting. Zoe joined the rest of the staff at the wide oak table in the center of the room.

"Hello," Mathias said with a stern face. "There is not much to update from the hospital, but things are unpredictable at the moment. For now, we will be in full cooperation with Detective Russo and her team as they look into the assault. Let's hope it does not escalate to a murder case."

Joanne gasped and then lowered her head. "Sorry, I…"

"No bother. This is a shock to us all. Murder and Umstead State Park are two things that do not belong in the same sentence under my watch. That being said, I'm proud of how both Clem and Zoe handled themselves today. Ernest, I also appreciate your help with the first responders at the gate. This meeting is simply to check-in and ensure that everybody is doing alright."

"We could use some extra staff for the time being," Zoe said. A louder, deeper voice in the room drowned her out.

"Can we get anybody on loan from Eno River?" Ernest asked without glancing at Zoe.

"I requested extra bodies, but Eno is already understaffed as it is. There is a level of concern that if we shift resources too heavily, our culprit may shift accordingly."

"Did the game cameras catch anything out there?" Zoe asked

"None were near the scene of the attack. Right, Ernest? How many did you get up yesterday?"

Ernest fiddled with his belt. "Two up by Big Lake, where the most recent sightings were. We got one up over by Sendero Gate, where we have seen people sneaking in after-hours for all kinds of mischief, but the signal went dark last night."

"How in the hell does that happen?" Clem asked.

"Weak batteries or somebody tampered with it. I'd imagine it's more the former than the latter, considering how well we hid that bad boy."

"Joanne, can you project your screen onto the monitor here and open the files that are in the different folders?"

Joanne nodded and buzzed off to set things up while the rangers discussed the fallout further.

"Is there still blood on the trail?" Zoe asked.

"Taken care of," Ernest said again without looking in her direction. Zoe tried to discern whether his evasiveness was any different from his usual blunt disdain for anybody different from himself.

Zoe added, "Thanks for doing that, Ernest. I planned to go back today and—"

Ernest raised a hand. "It's no bother, dear."

Zoe swallowed her growl at the unnecessary pet name and looked at Mathias, who nodded. Joanne interrupted by turning the monitor toward them. The bright screen emitted a light that was out of place in the dark mood of the room.

"Ernest was correct that there is nothing in Cam 1's folder.

That's the one that is over by Sendero gate. Cam 2 and 3 appear to have captured something though."

Mathias looked at Ernest. "Which is which?"

"Cam 2 is just off the trail, maybe ten yards. Cam 3 is down the social trail that the fisherman frequent but beyond their preferred spots to toss in a line. Didn't want to end up with thirty photos of Clem in his lawn chair losing the catch of the day."

Clem glared at Ernest but said nothing. He shifted his attention back to the monitor. Joanne had opened two photos from Cam 2, but nothing but a squirrel and a deer were in the frames so far. Zoe held her breath as Joanne clicked on the last one. Nothing in sight. Something obstructed the top corner of the frame, but they disregarded it as a leaf or branch. They moved on to Cam 3 and opened six photos of a deer navigating its way around a dried-out blueberry bush and a thicket of pine.

"Dang, well back to square one," Ernest muttered.

"Would it make sense to set one up by the, uh, by where Wade's body was?" Clem asked.

"We could. I see little merit in that, though. We need answers."

"Mathias, do you think there is a connection? To the sightings?" Clem said.

Mathias stroked his thumb on his cheek and paused. "No." The word bounced around the room like a pinball. Zoe watched as Joanne maneuvered the mouse to close each of the photos that were on the screen. She accidentally clicked to make one full screen instead, and it blew up on the wide monitor in front of them. Zoe almost jumped out of her seat.

"Look!" She pointed toward the screen.

"What? We looked at this one," Ernest said.

"In the background. Next to the Loblolly pine that is leaning at a forty-five-degree angle. Behind it."

Mathias moved his head towards the screen and squinted. "I don't see it."

Zoe couldn't take her eyes off the image. Just behind the half-downed trunk of a sweet gum tree was the outline of the back of a creature. It stood on two feet and facing away from the camera. "Is that..." she asked.

"Well, you wanted your answers, Mathias. Hope you're happy with what you've got," Ernest said with a tone dripped in sarcasm.

Mathias squinted at the screen and then slumped back into his chair. He turned to Zoe. "Anything else?"

"I've got somebody who may be able to help."

Ernest groaned. "Oh god, don't bring Silly Gilly into this mess."

"No, not Gil. He's compromised because he's the one who tipped off the authorities and drove us to put the cameras up. Somebody else."

"Gil did what now?" Ernest shouted.

"Drop it, Ernest," Mathias said in his leonine roar.

"My cousin is in town. She's a detective from up north. Her boyfriend is here too, and he's a private eye who specializes in stuff like this."

"In stuff like what?" Mathias growled.

"Supernatural. Spooky, unexplainable stuff." Nobody spoke, so Zoe pushed on. "I'm sorry for what Gil has done, but he meant no harm. And to be honest, we have bigger fish to fry now."

Clem stood from his chair. The blood had drained from his face as he continued to stare at the blown-up image on the screen. He turned and faced Zoe.

"Zoe, if you're looking at the same thing I am... well... that ain't no fish. *That's a god-damned ape!*"

CHAPTER SEVENTEEN

THE PHOTOS on the wall reflected the sunlight as it peeked through the window shades and made shadows on the drab, old wallpaper. The wallpaper looked more tan than the white color it had upon its installation, but somehow fit with the decor of the small cottage in the woods. It was clear that Zoe had spent considerably more time and effort making the place a home than she had when Delaney had first visited in the early days of Zoe's career as a ranger. It put Delaney's beachside shack to shame. She'd barely hung one framed photo on the wall and half of her books sat idly on bedside tables in stacks about to topple over.

Casper sat next to her on the couch and kept glancing back toward the front door. She sensed his nervousness and although she found it cute that he still had butterflies before taking on a case, still, it was her place to reinforce his wavering confidence.

She nudged Casper with her shoulder. "Hey, I can see the doubts forming in your mind. Have a little faith," she said.

"I know, I know. It's just—"

"You came out to the Cape with this bravado and swagger that was downright impressive."

"Yeah?"

"Oh no, wait. That was Hoagie. You awkwardly stumbled into my life, chasing after your wild-at-heart dog as it ran around an active crime scene."

"Always knew he'd be the reason I got a date someday."

On cue, Hoagie let out a howl and jumped onto the couch with a frisbee in his mouth. Casper tossed it down the hallway.

"Casper?"

"Yes, Detective Shepard?" Casper teased.

"I'm glad you awkwardly stumbled into my life. Just want to make that clear."

Casper blushed. "Thanks for bringing me down here. I'm having a lot of fun. You know… besides the assault and investigation and all."

"Glad you're by my side. Now, keep your chin up and stay confident. You've got a perspective that these rangers are lacking. They think they're looking for a beast in the woods. Steer them in the right direction."

Casper nodded, and the front door swung open. Zoe hurried through and plopped a stack of files onto the kitchen table. "Here's everything you wanted and then some."

"Can I ask a favor, Zoe?" Casper asked, approaching the heap of paperwork.

"Go for it. Only thing left on my morning agenda is to go yell at Gil for being a jerk. That can wait five minutes, I think. Is he even here?"

"He's been in his office since breakfast. Haven't heard a peep," Delaney said.

"Yeah, that happens. No reason to be alarmed. Let's hope he's making a dent in his manuscript. Anyway, what's up?"

"Let's start with the basics. How long have you been a ranger here?"

"Six years next February. Dang, feels like ages."

"And tell me a bit about the park?"

"Uh, well, do you want like acreage and history or the current state of things?"

"Let's start with the current state of things. The basics should do. Just trying to get myself acquainted."

"Well, we're the busiest park in all of North Carolina in terms of visitors. We're smack dab in the middle of Raleigh and Durham, so we get it from all angles. Most folks are here to run, hike, bike, or fish. Harmless stuff."

"And what's a normal week like?"

"Nothing to write home about. Patrolling parking lots to make sure nobody breaks into cars. Helping injured and lost hikers from time to time. Each ranger has an assignment that goes beyond their normal duties. Ernest is in charge of the horse trails that are all over the park. Clem is in charge of foot trails and diverting them when the tread gets too worn or washed out. I'm the volunteer coordinator, so I get to watch Boy Scout troops pick up trash and help church groups power wash the picnic tables."

"Short straw, eh?"

"So short there is barely any straw left. But you get the gist."

"And how many staff are there? I know I've met some, but-"

"Four rangers, which is about six rangers too few. But every park is understaffed. We've got support staff too. Joanne Mitchell is our office administrator. The maintenance crew is led by Henry Meise and he's got a few seasonal kids working under him."

"Okay, so Mathias is the boss?"

"Superintendent, technically. Took over for the highly respected Katie Pope when she accepted an NPS job at Shenandoah. He's the engine that keeps this place running in a lot of ways. Besides working, he's got a family at home and his wife is taking night classes to become a registered nurse. He sets everybody's schedules and tends to be fair. Not much peculiar about the man beside the unnecessary care he gives his Tom Selleck mustache and his aversion to speaking."

"And who is the next in line?"

"It doesn't exactly work like that, but that would probably be Ernest Henley. Older than the dirt on the trails. Former police officer and military man. He's got arthritis in both knees but still refuses to do any desk work. He's your typical grandpa type, and to this day I've never seen him without a hat on. It's glued to his head."

"Who else?"

"Clem Jenkins would be the fourth. If you run into him, don't mention that you're from the north. He'll start on his rant about the out-of-towners moving to the area that are ruining everything he likes about the Carolinas. He's a native, and if you hear him speak, you'll remember that with each slow-as-molasses word that seeps out of his lips."

"Seems like you're not a big fan?"

"He's an ass, but he's got some redeeming qualities. I think the sexist tendencies towards me and Joanne are an act that he's using to cover some insecurities. He works hard and takes his lumps when they come. I could ask for a much worse coworker when it's all said and done."

"Clem is the one that found the man on the trail?"

"Yup. Looked like a deer in headlights."

Casper nodded. "Okay, changing gears. In the past few years, has anything peculiar like this happened?"

"Like this? No, sir."

"Anything out of the ordinary, I guess."

"I mean, Clem arrested a man who had a joint on him two years back. That had him buzzing for the next six months. We had two break-ins outside the visitor's center, but that's not that out of the ordinary. We had suspicions that there were hand-to-hand drug deals taking place in the parking lots, but that lost traction too. Then maybe six months ago, the sightings started up."

"And have they been steady? More frequent?"

"Initially, it was rare. We'd get a spooked hiker recounting their harrowing tale in great detail, but we thought little of it. Being so close to Durham and Raleigh, we get lots of folks who don't know what they don't know. They come in saying they just saw a Sasquatch, but it was actually just the backside of a deer."

"So, they gave the sightings little credibility at that point?"

"Until this morning, they had zero credibility. I'd come home and tell Gil about it, and he'd get all riled up. Beyond that, nothing was out of the ordinary at the park. After the first few, Ernest put up a map on the bulletin board in the back office and we started putting pins where people saw things. Might as well be one of those light-bulb screens we played with as kids. What was that called, Laney?"

"Lite-Brite. Oh, man, we'd spend hours playing with that thing!"

"Feel like we should bust that out when this mess clears up. I'll see if they've got one on Amazon to get here ASAP."

"Okay, last few questions. Up for it?" Casper asked. "I hate to interrupt the reminiscing."

"No, this is important. Bring it on."

"What's the approach now? You said that Gil tipped somebody off and things escalated. What does that mean?"

"Mathias, my boss, had his hand forced by somebody above him to take action. So, we planned to print out informational posters for the public and hang them around the bathrooms. That and Ernest put up a few game cameras. They're motion activated, so it snaps a photo each time something nearby moves."

"Right, and these cameras provided the photo you mentioned? Can you send me a copy of that?"

Zoe tapped her palm on the stack of files. "Right here for you. It's grainy to put it gently. I doubt it'll be of much use, but we had four skeptics in a room and everybody agreed it was Bigfoot-like."

"Great. I'll take a look. One last question for you." Casper leaned in towards her. "What's your take? If you had to explain this, what's your guess?"

"Eh, I don't know if I'm the right—"

"Zo, you know this park like the playground in your parent's backyard. Don't be humble. Use that noggin of yours and tell my boyfriend your best crackpot theory!" Delaney said with a grin.

Zoe sighed. "If I *had* to guess. Somebody is doing all of this to scare up the town. They were putting on a show this morning and ran into Wade Buchanon. Wrong place, wrong time. Beat him to keep him quiet."

Casper nodded. "That's logical. A connecting of the dots. Thank you. I'll circle back with you once I've had time to review these files, but maybe later tonight."

"I think we all could benefit from some time off later, but let's see how the night goes. For now, I need to go yell at my fiancé. So, plug your ears," Zoe hugged Delaney then stormed off to the back bedroom.

"What do you think about all this, Laney?" Casper asked.

"Laney is a childhood nickname. Don't think that I forgot that your middle name is Archie, so watch it with the name-calling."

Casper grinned. "Anyway, your theory?"

Delaney stood and paced around the tiny kitchen table. "This is weird. Somehow more bizarre than what happened up at the Cape. There seems to be some level of absurdity that follows you around, Casper Kelly. But I dig it. I dig it."

"To me, I'm struck by the motive. Scaring people into thinking that Bigfoot is real doesn't feel like enough of a reason to beat somebody up. It doesn't even feel like enough of a motive to dress up in a costume and parade around the park grounds either. Greed or fear usually motivates people. So, I'd start with greed and see what pops."

"You mean, like somebody who is writing a book about the same creature that is all of a sudden popping up around town?" Casper asked with a lump in his throat.

"Better to clear his name now and get out in front of it. Otherwise, Zoe's life is about to be flipped upside down."

On cue, Zoe's roar seeped through the crack under the bedroom door as she grilled her hapless author of a fiancé. Delaney faked a smile and pointed towards the stack of files. "Maybe we dig into these on the back deck?"

CHAPTER EIGHTEEN

CLOTHES FLEW AROUND the room like a child playing dress-up. Zoe sat on the bed trying to convince Gil's temper to simmer down, but he continued to rage. Her attempts to confront him about his lack of consideration in his decision-making were fool-hearted. Gil had always been sensitive and the brutal events of the day had blinded Zoe's senses. She had ripped into him with all the fury that she'd saved up from countless long lectures on how she needed more patience with his work.

"You believe I am responsible for this? For these sightings? For this morning's crime? Zoe, I—"

"Just calm—"

"I know I have been working significant hours as of late, but put my career on hold for this book. I do not enjoy middling through book advances without meeting the deadlines. It is quite stressful! We cannot all be desk-duty park rangers, Zoe!"

"Drop that tone. That's bullshit and you know it. I simply asked if you knew more than you were letting on about the recent rash of sightings in the park. I didn't—"

"And you think I beat that man within an inch of his life?" Gil scoffed and snatched a shirt from the closet. "What kind of monster do you think I am?"

"Gil, I—"

"Next you are going to ask me if I am a serial killer, right?"

"Gil, that's quite a leap. I don't—"

"One small step for man. One giant leap for Bigfoot enthusiasts everywhere," Gil said as he stuffed a sweater into his bag and ripped the zipper shut.

"Stop. You're being ridiculous. Just take a second to breathe and—"

"Breathe?" His face turned as red as the sky during a sunset. "How am I supposed to breathe? You are here accusing me of a small catalog of crimes and then telling me to calm down. That, as you would say, is bullshit, Zoe. I know I can be cold but-"

"Gil, I simply asked you a question and—"

Gil glared at her. "If you trusted me, you wouldn't have to ask such a thing." He stormed out.

Zoe sat on the bed. Gil's car started and then sped off down the road. She let out a deep breath and turned back to face Delaney and Casper on the back porch.

Casper kept his gaze on the files, but Delaney stood to comfort her. "Want to talk about it?"

Zoe nodded. "There's not a lot to say. I had dug into him before you came about calling in the tip, and I just wanted to once again explain my point of view. But he blew up. He's always had a temper, but usually it's self-destructive. I don't know what to do now."

"Wait him out. Not much more you can do besides wait for him to process everything and come back. I know you feel that you screwed up, but no more than he did," Delaney said. "Let's get some drinks and forget this awful day ever happened. It's almost five. You have the day off, remember?"

"Yeah but-"

"But what?"

"That felt like an overreaction to me. I thought I knew him, but..."

"Are you interpreting an overreaction as an indicator of guilt? I don't think he seems like a violent man, but you—"

"No, that's what makes no sense." Zoe shook her head and slumped into a chair. "I don't think he'd ever be violent or lash out. Especially not toward a stranger."

"Well, good then. Try to relax."

"But he's hiding something... I just don't know what it is."

Casper gulped and summoned his bravest face. "It may be time that I mention something else that came up in my initial review of the case."

"Let's hear it," Delaney said.

Casper tapped the stack of file folders that stood in two piles. "Well, first I wanted to view the assault and the sightings as isolated incidents. Circles without an overlap in their Venn diagram. When taking that approach, the sightings are a conundrum." He paused and looked at Zoe. "There are few people who would stand to benefit from such incidents."

Zoe nodded and let out an exhale. "You mean like a researcher writing a book on the subject area?"

Casper bit his bottom lip and nodded. Zoe stared at ice cubes in her drink, as if waiting for them to melt and turn into water. A new form. To Casper, humans didn't feel all that different. Under the right conditions, people change into something unrecognizable. If the Punkhorns had taught him anything, that much was true.

"Okay. Let's check his office. He's run off in a huff, so we've got a few hours at least." Zoe stood. "Best-case scenario, we find nothing incriminating."

"Worst-case scenario?" Delaney asked.

"Let's not go there just yet." Zoe led them down the hallway and used the flathead key that sat on the top of the doorway to unlock the door. Hoagie nudged himself in and plopped onto the floor, panting from an extended stretch of time in the sun.

"He locks his office?"

"Sometimes." She fiddled with the lock and then pushed the door open. "He said it's just out of habit from when he had an office at the university. I've never had a reason to come in here, anyway."

The stench of stale coffee and old notebooks hit them the second they entered. Zoe pointed over towards the desk that held his laptop. She moved the mouse, and it came to life.

"You know the password?" Delaney said.

"I used to know it. But it may take a guess or two."

After two attempts, Zoe typed one last guess in and the screen flickered and opened to a browser. Gil's email was on the screen, but the inbox was empty.

"Anything over there?" Zoe asked Casper, who was sorting through a stack of file folders with handwritten labels. Casper shook his head. "No, just old files from his research, it looks like. Nothing within the last year or so."

"Check his trash," Delaney said.

Zoe hesitated. "This feels wrong. I don't-"

"Would it feel better if I did it?"

"Somehow, yeah, it would," Zoe said and switched spots with Delaney.

With a click, Delaney brought up Gil's discarded messages, but only three were on the screen. "Either he doesn't get much email or he sets them to auto-delete after a certain time period. There are two here from a book cover contractor about drafts for the paperback edition of his novel. The other seems to be from his publisher."

Delaney clicked on the message. Zoe turned away.

"What's it say, Laney?"

Zoe watched as Delaney's eyes read the message once and then read over it again. She gulped.

"It says that considering the recent sightings, the publisher has an interest in a second contract with him. A follow up to his current novel."

Casper interrupted. "As somebody who has dealt with editors when I wrote a book many years ago, I don't know how much we should read into this."

"How so?"

"They work to keep all their options open. This is nothing more than an initial mention of it. But it's still a grim look for Gil's innocence. His motive just got stronger."

"But hear me out. If he's responsible for the sightings, well, that is one thing. As long as he's not the one responsible for the assault, he's still just an idiot in the woods," Delaney said.

"For sure. There's no link right now besides peculiar timing," Casper said.

"No, there's something else," Zoe interrupted. "We heard from the crime lab just before I got home for the day. They confirmed they found animal fur on and around the wounds. They're running more tests to determine the specifics but it'll be days before we hear anything from the county crime lab."

"Oh, no. Zo-"

"It's okay. We still have time to piece this together. I'm just glad we know now. But let's keep this between us for now? I don't want to let Detective Russo know about any of this until I can talk with Gil and get some answers."

Casper and Delaney nodded. The mood in the room had taken a somber turn. Zoe led them out, locked the door, and placed the key back in its spot. In the hallway, she leaned against the wall and took in a deep breath. *Gil, what the hell have you done?*

CHAPTER NINETEEN

THE ATHLETIC FIELDS of Pine Hills High School sat within a half-mile-wide stretch of grass surrounded by a rickety rusted fence. Persistent teenagers had ripped holes in the fence that bordered the neighborhoods. Officials had re-attached the fence with great care, only to find it busted open again in a matter of hours.

A janitor zoomed through the border of the field on a riding lawn mower, kicking up blades of grass and the fresh-cut smell that would forever remind Kyle of early morning runs and cross-country courses. Two fields, each bookended with silver goalposts enclosed by an orange net, were full of teenagers chasing a soccer ball like it was the last dinner roll at supper. Chaos was unfolding. The coaches paid little mind.

As Kyle cleared the top step that led to the lot, he saw Andy off with the smaller of the two teams. He maneuvered past the Varsity team's practice. A defender dashed to catch their striker, only to resort to a nasty slide tackle that put three bodies on the ground. Their coach wasn't watching. Kyle could see him fumbling with his canister of dip, trying to form another pinch.

Andy's team was running wind-sprints, either as punishment or because there wasn't anything better to do than to get them into shape. Andy watched, arms crossed on top of his chest.

He noticed Kyle approach, blew the whistle, and the entire team dropped to the ground. Each athlete's hands were on their knees, back bent as they gasped for air. A few of Kyle's students waved at him as he approached, but he didn't acknowledge their presence, nor did they do much more than look his way. He wasn't there to check up on the JV Soccer team or scold somebody for plagiarism on their essay. He was there to tell Andy the bad news.

"You look like complete shit," Andy said.

"Didn't you read any of my texts?" Kyle glared at him. "I need to talk to you."

Andy shrugged. "I had my kids until this morning and then had practice. I figured you knew. It's the exact reason you took on that job for me and—"

"Yeah, that's why I needed to talk to you."

Andy met Kyle's stare. His smile disappeared. "Did something happen?" His eyes grew wide. "Oh, shit. Did you get caught?"

"Would I be here without handcuffs if I got caught?"

"I don't know how the criminal justice system works. I've seen a lot of Law and Order and usually they try to flip somebody who has information."

"What information do I have for them?" Kyle raised his voice. The students all looked their way.

Andy turned toward the team. "You all meet up with the Varsity now on the other field. I'll be up in a minute." He put a hand on Kyle's shoulder. "Just need to chat with Mr. Pittman about which one of us will chaperone Junior Prom."

The kids milled about and made their way toward the adjoining field where the Seniors were running drills. Andy watched them before speaking again.

"Is this the part where I check if you're wearing a wire?"

"Feel free. But after you're done inspecting my abs, we can talk about the serious shit that went down yesterday."

"Yeah? From the text seemed like a normal drop..."

"Drop was a piece of cake. Simple spot to find. But I got curious afterward."

"You what?" Andy's stare was icy.

Kyle looked at the grass as he spoke. "I made the drop and then hid in the woods to see who came to pick it up."

"Oh, shit. Kyle-"

Kyle raised his hand. "Don't. I know it's against the code and the rules and whatever else you're going to throw at me. It was a mistake. I promise you."

"So, what happened? Some skin and bones teen come and take the backpack after you left?"

"Much, much worse."

"How do you mean worse?" Andy whispered.

"I saw The Fox."

"You what?" Andy shouted.

Kyle looked around and was thankful nobody was nearby. "I saw The Fox. No doubt about it. I hung around for fifteen minutes and The Fox came and picked up my delivery."

"How do you know it was him?"

"First off, the person was in a life-sized fox costume. Like, the shit you see at Disney World or something. But they were smaller. It was a human."

"Oh damn, Kyle. You had me going for a minute." Andy roared with laughter. "Dang. You're a talented actor. You know that?"

Kyle grabbed Andy's arm. "I'm not joking, man. And I'm not done with my story."

"Okay, let's hear it."

"The Fox came, picked up the backpack, but while I watched that go down, somebody ran down the hill. This middle-aged dude in short shorts and bright blue shoes. The Fox saw him approach and ducked under the bridge."

"Okay…"

"But this dude. The old guy. He must have seen The Fox hide because he slowed to a walk and then called out." Kyle's eyes grew panicked. "The Fox shot out of the hiding spot and was on top of the guy in seconds. The dude tried to block the blows with his arms, but The Fox was relentless. Manic. Dude, blood was everywhere."

"What the f—"

"So, I snap myself out of the daze I'm in and I decide to book it. The last thing I want is for The Fox to see me there, watching this man get beat to a pulp. But I stumble and make a noise."

"A noise?"

"A branch on the forest floor cracked. I looked back at the trail and saw The Fox there. No longer wailing on the poor dude that walked up. Now, The Fox was staring into the woods. Right at me. And then, The Fox pulled off their mask and waved at me."

"Waved at you?"

"Yeah. Like just letting me know they saw me. Some seriously sick shit. Who dresses up like an animal and lurks around the park? Who has that much rage inside of them they'd beat a stranger like that?" Kyle paced around the sideline. "Dude, I'm so done. I'm out."

"What do you mean you're out?"

"I mean, I'm not taking jobs for The Fox anymore. You can have them all. Buy your kids tickets to Disneyland for all I care. Just leave me out of it from here on out."

Andy crossed his arms. "And what if The Fox asks about you? According to this story, you know what The Fox looks like and maybe the only person—"

"I was far out in the woods. It was still before sunrise. I think it was all a mind game. Like, The Fox just waved into the woods to scare the shit out of whoever was there."

"But you saw what they looked like?"

Kyle gulped and nodded.

"So, what's stopping you from going to the police?"

"The police? Dude, what am I supposed to say? I saw a cartoon-ishly large fox beat a man senseless because I had just hidden drugs there as part of my illicit part-time job?"

"Maybe leave some of that out but—"

"No way. They don't have witness protection for two-bit drug runners. I'd be in the system and out of a job. My life would be over. I'm just walking away. Clean slate."

"Brother, your slate is far from clean, but I hear you. I just don't know how that will work."

"I'm only here to tell you because it was your job. And I thought I should warn you."

Andy froze. "Warn me? Why?"

In the silence, Kyle could almost hear the gears click into place in Andy's brain as he sorted through the situation at hand.

He put his hands over his eyes. "Oh, holy shit. If they couldn't see that well from a distance, The Fox might suspect that the person in the woods was a certain someone who had a reason to be there. Like me, who had just dropped drugs under the bridge under orders from The Fox."

"Yeah."

"Holy shit. You may have just gotten me killed, Kyle Pittman. What the f—"

Kyle put both hands on Andy's shoulders and looked him straight in the eyes. "I never meant for any of this to come back on you." He spoke slowly. "Let me figure out what to do next and I'll keep you in the loop. I just thought you should know, so you could watch your back."

"This is bad news, man." Andy shook his head. "I've got kids! They can't walk into their daddy's room and find him beaten within an inch of his life."

"I'll figure something out. Just give me some time. Okay?"

"Keep me updated. I'll do the same. But otherwise, I'm going to try and act normal. If The Fox is watching, I don't want to act suspicious. I'll just keep teaching and coaching and—"

"Yeah, keep it up. You did nothing wrong. Hang in there, man."

Andy shook his head. "Damn, Kyle."

"I know, Andy. I know."

CHAPTER TWENTY

THE CREAK of old seat springs echoed through the tiny bedroom. Casper flashed one eye open and then the other. He reached back towards Delaney's side of the bed but found nothing but a cold pillow. The creak sounded again. Followed by a sincere sigh.

"I thought I'd be able to do this without waking you up," Delaney said. She sat cross-legged with a stack of files on her lap. Hoagie lay at her feet, chewing on a toy.

"Can't go sneaking around like that. Scared me half to death," Casper said.

Delaney mouthed the word 'sorry' and then dove back into the files.

"Find anything interesting?"

"Nothing to exonerate Gil. He's still got the best motive for the Bigfoot sightings, but that's only an issue if the dots connect to Wade Buchanon."

"And what are the dots telling you at this ungodly hour of the morning?"

"The dots request coffee before speaking further. I agree with the dots."

"Before coffee, I need to ask you something," Casper said. He spoke quickly, afraid to run out of steam or courage in the moment. "What does *Raven Rock* mean?"

Delaney's face flushed red. She dropped the files and closed her eyes. After a deep breath, she faked a smile. "Where did you hear that?"

"Somebody mentioned it."

"Well, that somebody was sticking their nose where it didn't belong." She glared at him. "Did you go digging into my past, Casper?"

He shook his head. "No, I swear. I came home to a random note on my door in Brewster. It told me to ask you about Raven Rock."

She let out a half-laugh that bordered on a whimper. "Figures. Can't escape my past even if I moved across the world."

"So?"

Delaney sighed. "I don't think I'm ready to talk about this with you. I... well, it's complicated and for the moment, we're on vacation. Can we pretend we never had this chat?"

"I can try."

She met his eyes. "I know you're stubborn, so I'll give you this much. It's an old case from a millennium before I met you or Hoag or moved to Brewster. It belongs in the past, so I try to keep it there as much as possible."

He nodded. "So, coffee?" She faked a smile and then marched out of the door. Alone with his misery and doubts, Casper got dressed. Delaney stood in the kitchen, arms crossed like she was angry at the sun. She poured beans into the grinder and created the magical aroma that Casper associated with his old loft in Brewster.

"Nice to see Zoe sleeping in a bit. Unless she's out looking for Gil," Casper said, desperate for a change of subject that would ease the tension of the room.

"No, I'm up." Zoe entered the kitchen in full uniform. "You're not the only early birds in the house, ya know."

"How's your head?" Delaney asked with a grin.

"Just fine, Laney. Do you think I've become a lightweight in my old age or something? I could still drink you under the table. Just be happy that I didn't bust out the moonshine."

"Moonshine? Embracing your southern home, eh?"

"Sam Jordan keeps me stocked up. Just a friendly guy who loves to fish at the park, but damnit if the muscadine moonshine is not poison in a glass. That'll knock your socks off."

"Any word from Gil?" Casper asked.

"Not a thing. I was thinking, Delaney... do you know anybody in law enforcement that would do me a favor and track his phone?"

Delaney pressed the start button on the coffeemaker and turned back to face her cousin. "I know you're worried when you call me by my full name. But no need to involve law enforcement. I can do you one better."

"Oh yeah?"

"I'll work some magic later and let you know what I find."

Zoe smiled. "Thanks, Del."

"But I can assure you, he's okay. Probably shacked up in a hotel watching old footage of Bigfoot sightings and crying for being such a fool."

"That... is not a sight I needed this early in the morning. It'll be a long day, so I'll need extra coffee."

"What's the plan today?" Casper asked.

"I was about to ask you the same thing."

Casper mulled it over. "In my eyes, we've been reactive so far. Working off the clues left behind. Maybe it's time we make a move of our own."

"As in?"

"You said the spot where the camera caught our friend on film is dense, right? Let's set up camp there tonight."

"Like a trap?"

"More or less," Casper said. "Do you think you could get Mathias to go for that?"

Zoe grinned. "Much like my little cousin there, I believe I can be mighty persuasive when I need to be."

"Can we join?" Delaney asked.

"I'll ask. I don't see why he'd say no to bringing another LEO as some backup. Casper will be the harder sell. He asked that I bring you over to the Visitor's Center with me this morning so you two can touch base. Mind if I steal him, Laney?"

"With pleasure. I need some time to myself, anyway. Mind if I take Hoagie and run the trails while you two save the world?"

"Only if you're extra careful. I hear some dangerous creatures are roaming around the park these days," Zoe said. Nobody laughed.

Mathias Wittles had his jet-black hair combed so neatly it looked like it was hand drawn. His icy stare had followed Casper from the second he entered, fierce light blue eyes that exuded confidence and skepticism. He waved Zoe in and she ushered Casper along. They plopped themselves into two old chairs with worn cushions. The room smelled like mulch and stale coffee.

"It's a pleasure to meet you, sir. I'm Casper Kelly."

Mathias nodded. "Welcome to our park, Mr. Kelly."

Zoe cleared her throat. "I know I didn't sell you on his services yesterday but…"

"You thought maybe a good night's sleep knocked some sense into me?" He grinned.

Zoe shrugged. "To be honest, sometimes I feel like I'm the only one trying to solve this case."

Mathias grinned. "That is because this is not a case, Zoe. Particularly not one of ours. You can submit whatever information you'd like to Detective Russo, who is in charge of the assault. I'd imagine she'd even sit down and walk you through what they have so far. It would take all of thirty seconds."

"So the police don't have anything either," Casper said.

Mathias glared at him. "Look, I appreciate that you are here and in town. Explore the park. Hike around. I'm sorry if you've been misinformed, but we have no interest in outside resources. I thought I made that clear enough to Zoe. Additionally, we will not expend any additional internal resources on this either."

"Mathias, we have to figure out what's going on. We—"

He raised his hand. "Mr. Kelly. Can you give us a minute?"

Casper nodded and ducked out of the room. Through the closed door, he could hear the raised voice of Mathias scolding Zoe for her lack of respect for authority and her over-earnest nature. When Zoe slinked out, she looked like a high schooler that just got a week-long detention from the principal. He followed her out front where she stood with her hands on her hips.

"I'm sorry, Casper," she said. "I shouldn't have lied to you. I thought once Mathias saw you and met you... well, I'm sorry."

Casper nodded. "It was worth a try. I've seen many men like Mathias. They're set in their ways. The *this is how we've always done it* crowd. It's frustrating during a case; I can't even imagine working with him every day."

"It sucks, but that's nothing new. But I just know that he's wrong."

Casper raised a brow. "Wrong?"

"There's something out there. And I'll be damned if I rest while it harms another innocent person. Tell me, what would you do?"

Casper watched a hawk dive into the thick canopies that surrounded the parking lot. Squirrels hopped around in the brush, collecting the last few nuts they'd need for a long winter ahead. He watched Zoe, who kicked rocks with her feet and kept her gaze fixed on the ground. "The only thing that will move this case forward and into the view of folks like Mathias... is proof."

"Proof?"

"Verifiable proof. More than a blurry photograph."

"So?"

"So, I think it's about time we set our trap."

CHAPTER TWENTY-ONE

A RED CLOUDLESS sky followed Zoe's truck as she and Casper drove home to prepare for the evening's risky plan. Despite her initial confidence in the idea, she had started to waver at the prospect of capturing such a wild creature. A creature still wasn't likely, but it was a possibility. One that she hoped they'd walk out of the woods able to eliminate.

Delaney had wrapped up her run and driven to grab a shower, so Casper hopped in with Zoe to hitch a ride back to the house. Her truck's stereo belted out a familiar tune that had taken on an ominous similarity to the mess at hand. *Bad Moon Rising* blared through the speakers. "You a fan?" She asked Casper, who hummed along in the passenger seat.

He nodded. "Except when I was a kid, I always thought they were saying *there's a bathroom on the right.*"

Zoe chuckled. "Like somebody giving directions?"

"Yup. It wasn't until high school that I actually learned the words," Casper smiled and sang along with the chorus. *"Don't go around tonight. Well, it's bound to take your life. There's a bad moon on the rise."*

Zoe smiled and made a mental note to tell Delaney she'd chosen well. But the lyrics hit differently without Gil nearby. With so much uncertainty around the park. Around her job. Around her life. There certainly was a bad moon on the rise. Zoe watched Casper picking at his fingers and cleared her throat. "Something on your mind? Not impressed with our park?"

Casper smiled. "No, it's mighty nice. Something else. I guess with everything going on with you and Gil, I'm starting to wonder how well I know Delaney."

"She's an open book for the most part."

"I thought so too. But I'm thinking that some pages may be missing. Specifically about Raven Rock."

"Raven Rock, eh?"

"Does that mean something to you?"

"The past was a complicated time for her. There's a lot there that even I don't know. But let me ask you, do you have any skeletons in your closet?"

Casper shook his head. "None that I'm hiding."

Zoe sighed. "That's great. Some of us aren't so lucky."

"So, how do I get her to open up?"

"If she's anything like me, the more you press her, the harder she'll buck. Give her space and earn your trust."

Casper chuckled. "Noted."

"But take my advice with a grain of salt. I might have had Gil all wrong."

"How so?"

Zoe paused for a moment. "No use in dragging that lake right now. Let's just crack this case and find some answers."

Between the pines that lined the entrance road, Zoe squinted then frowned. The driveway held her beat-up gray Prius with the hail damage on the roof and Delaney's grimy Subaru hatchback.

Something turned over in her stomach. For the first time, she worried about Gil's safety.

In past fights, Gil would often clam up and turn introspective in times that required self-examination or reflection. He wasn't the kind of man that processed things with speed or with others. That was fine with Zoe. Not everybody could know in a split-second how to respond or feel like she could. She'd let her gut betray her in this circumstance with Mathias and feared that her relationship with Gil would never recover, so who was she to talk?

DELANEY SAT on the front steps and waved to them as Zoe steered into the driveway.

"Remember when you asked me to try and locate Gil?" Delaney asked.

"Hello to you too, dear cousin."

All business, Delaney continued, "Well, I just worked my magic. I know where he is."

"I'm afraid to even ask. Do I want to know?"

"A good magician does not reveal their secrets."

"Of course." Zoe ran a jerky hand through her hair. "I need to know. Where is he? Is he at that motel off Hillsborough Street? He's hunkered down there before to work on his writing. I swear—"

"He's here," Delaney interrupted.

Zoe glanced into the windows of her humble cottage. No signs of movement. "Here?"

"Not *here* here. But it looks like he's somewhere in the park. The signal isn't exact, so there is a certain range that he could be within, but all signs point to him being somewhere inside the park boundaries."

Zoe plopped herself on the stairs and let her brain work over the recent information. Gil had run, but he stayed. Here. Within the park. Her heart followed her brain as they both worked at a feverish pace to sort through the details. "Delaney?" she asked, not sure if it was her heart or her brain talking.

"What's up?"

"I... uh... can I share something in confidence?"

"Always, Zo. Remember how incredible I was at keeping secrets as a kid? I'm even better now."

"Okay, well, uh, Gil had been staying up at all hours of the night."

"And..."

"Well, I've been sleeping like a rock and don't hear him come and go from the bed. I just assume he's found a moment of inspiration for his work."

"Okay, so? I don't see the reason for this level of secrecy."

"So, I can't say unequivocally that Gil was next to me in bed all of Friday night and into Saturday morning."

"You think that—"

"No," Zoe waved her hand. "I don't think it. Just putting the evidence out there. It felt wrong to hold that in with this additional evidence. He's on the run. Missing. And now we know he's inside the park. And like you and Casper said, he has the most to gain from any Bigfoot related news. Literally the only person with something to gain, as far as I can tell..."

"Zoe, I—"

"Just let me process out loud for a second."

Delaney nodded.

"Gil is not an evil man. I'm certain of that much at least. He's never shown a shred of violent tendencies or any real volatility. He's gentle. Predictable. But he's also desperate. I've watched this book deal weigh on him and the mounting pressure of his deadline cripple any enthusiasm he had left. It's changed him. I... well... I don't think he's in his right mind."

Delaney stood. "Zo, let me ask you flat out. Do you think Gil is responsible for all of this?"

Zoe's mind flashed images of Wade Buchanon's bloody torso

on the trail. The trail that was less than half a mile from their house. A path Gil knew as well as anybody. Better than most. But her gut rejected the notion. Something didn't fit. A square peg in a round hole.

"No. I don't think so. In my gut, I'm certain he's innocent. But, well, he's got some explaining to do to say the least."

Delaney sighed. "Look, at some point, it may be worth recusing yourself from the case. If you get too close—"

"Laney, this park is my home. Sure, it's a job that some days I hate and dread putting on the uniform, but I've lived here for most of my adult life. I've been too close. I am too close to this case. Every piece of it. But I'm not putting this in somebody else's hands. Not when we have an opportunity for answers tonight."

Delaney hugged her cousin. "Let's get dinner started so we can head out to the site."

Casper listened to their conversation through the door but kept his gaze fixed on a very sleepy Hoagie who was sprawled on the hardwood floor. Every instinct Casper had told him to help, but it was too easy to overstep in a family matter. Instead, he tried to keep his head down and find a clue to bring forth answers.

In a moment alone, Casper nudged Delaney with his shoulder and leaned in close. "So, how'd you track Gil?"

She smirked. "How would you have done it, Mr. Private Eye?"

Casper thought for a second and a memory flashed in his mind. "Probably through the Find my iPhone app on Gil's computer."

Delaney bit her lip, shook her head and smiled. "Maybe, maybe not."

After dinner, Zoe went to her room to throw on camouflage and black clothes to blend into her surroundings. She met Casper and Delaney in the living room and they kissed Hoagie goodnight. Zoe led them down the trail towards the game camera that had spotted the blurry figure. The walk was quiet and colored by the fiery sky of an early autumn sunset. After an hour, they were at the spot.

The mist sparkled in the moonlight and settled around the leaves that had fallen from overhead branches early in the season. Shadows flickered. The slightest movement was like an orchestra beginning to play. Zoe could hear little else besides her heartbeat and the rhythm of her chest rising and falling with her breath. Her frigid breath fogged in a cloud in front of her in the pale light from above.

Three hours in, little else besides a tiny four-legged critter had scampered across their path. Chipmunk. The breeze picked up and Zoe wondered if it was wind or just the hunting party breathing a collective sigh of relief. As much as they wanted answers, nobody seemed prepared for the aftermath of any possible discovery.

Casper had split the three of them into quadrants, with the empty corner being the neighboring roadway. He helped find the best vantage point for each. Delaney sat with her back on a rotted stump facing the rest of them. Casper's corner had a slight incline, and he parked himself at its peak with an optimal view down into the valley below. Zoe's perch was on a pile of fallen dogwoods and loblolly pines that resembled a graveyard.

Each of the others were invisible to Zoe when they were still. The darkness came upon them and swallowed each of them into the night. The moonlight was dim, and the stars did little to provide a spotlight into the surrounding forest. Zoe grew restless. Then the restlessness passed and the exhaustion from the weekend set in. Her eyelids grew heavy. Drooped down despite Zoe's best fight. But as they touched down and closed out the little light that remained around her, a noise sounded. A crunch of leaves. In the distance. Her eyes shot open. Darting around but saw nothing.

The noise sounded again. The earlier sounds of squirrels and chipmunks were pitter patters of tiny feet hopping through the woods. This sound was larger. Like an earthquake when it came. Unmistakable. It was a footstep.

CHAPTER TWENTY-TWO

AN AIRPLANE FLEW low over the rooftops and rattled the three ice cubes melting in Andy's glass. His second pour of Cuervo, three fingers this time, sat undisturbed as Andy picked at his fingernails and tapped his leg on the ground, trying to keep his focus on the TV. A cell phone vibrated on the desk and snatched his full attention away from the passing aircraft and the reruns of *How I Met Your Mother.* He glanced at the screen. He'd hoped it would be Kyle checking in or even an angry message from Regina cursing him out for yesterday's snafu with the kids. But none of that was in the cards. The contact name was a fox emoji.

He held the phone in front of him and paced around his condo's tiny kitchen as he debated his next move. The message was open. It was right there and waiting for him. It might as well have been dollar signs in place of the fox emoji, because that's all it meant. But the thought made Andy's heart race like when he'd first seen Regina in that crappy piano karaoke bar. Right before she went on stage and sang his favorite Billy Joel song. Right before a rushed wedding, two kids, and a quick divorce. *So much for 'The Longest Time,' Billy.*

Andy tipped the glass up and the cool, smooth liquid coated his throat as he gulped it down. He put the phone in the other room while he looked over his savings account and poured another glass. The balance was healthy, something he'd worked hard for. Something he'd bent the law for. Broke his back for. Everything. All the small transfers added up. Still, there was an instinct inside that clamored for more. More safety. More security. More to prove Regina wrong.

He swiped at the message, and a wave of relief washed over him. He read through the instructions. *Phew, okay. Normal job. Different coordinates, but nothing out of the ordinary.* Andy wrote the details on a notepad and responded as he always did with just two letters. "OK".

He tossed the phone and fixed his eyes back on the TV. Ted Mosby was moping about some girl that was *definitely* the one yet was sure to end up a disaster. The phone vibrated again. Andy's stomach turned over. He glanced at the screen and his mouth went dry. It was The Fox. Again.

The process, which was spelled out with no wasted words in the initial email, was that there would be one text with the instructions. The runner copies down the information, deletes the message, and the check hits the bank within twenty-four hours of a completed job. One message. Not two. Not in a row.

He read the second message. *"Leave the contents out. Hide it in plain view. Burn the bag."*

Andy's heart fluttered. The hairs on the back of his neck stood up like a dog frightened by a threat. He sorted through all the possibilities in his head that he could come up with. He called Kyle. Voicemail again. He left another.

"Kyle, it's me, man. Our friend just messaged. I'm feeling twisted about this, dude. After what you saw. After what you told me. Now, I'm getting two messages. I feel like it's a trap. Like, like I'm the fall guy. Oh, dude, I've seen shit like this go down on CSI.

I'll be behind bars within an hour. But I also can't say no! That check. That money. Plus, there's more and—"

The voicemail beeped and Andy tossed his phone. He combed through his memories and tried to remember if he had ever seen Kyle without his phone. The unusual circumstance put a shiver down his spine like a cold winter's night. Something had changed in Kyle over the past few weeks. The once jovial, relaxed friend had become irritable, paranoid, and suspicious of everything. Andy wrote it off as girl trouble.

Last school year and into this summer, Kyle would recount his dating woes and swipe-right problems in great detail. Then, he said he met an older woman and stopped opening up about that side of his life. Andy had seen the impact that a breakup can have on a man firsthand. He knew the fallout from his divorce took years to come back from. Maybe Kyle was living something similar.

He checked the clock. The instructions provided a strict deadline. There was barely a half-hour left for Andy to get dressed and make his way towards the park.

THE FAMILIAR TEN-MINUTE drive was haunting. Shadows danced beneath street lights and revealed shapes that deceived his eyes. Everything was watching him. Passengers of other cars. Dogs on leashes. Stoplight cameras. A lump grew in his throat that ached for another shot of tequila. He swallowed the lump down and veered off the highway, onto the side road he'd parked countless times before. There wasn't a single car in sight. The small turnoff was public knowledge and often used by evening runners that wanted to avoid getting a ticket on their car for staying after hours. For Andy, it was the launching point for many of his late-night side jobs.

Outside of the car, he pulled on a black knit winter hat and jogged toward the trail. His muscles whined with every step, calves screeching for a proper warm-up routine. The overhead light on the distant street corner served as a spotlight as he bolted down the makeshift foot trail and entered the dark abyss that was Umstead State Park at night. A bare, moonless sky above provided little guidance, so Andy relied on his phone. The coordinates weren't far from the side access road that he'd started from, and within minutes he'd found a small backpack. He put on a pair of cloth gloves and felt the contents through the bag but couldn't discern what they were. The Fox was consistent in clever hiding spots that provided at least some level of assurance.

With the drop spot plugged into the app, he was off and running. Two miles as the crow flies became further as he cut through switchbacks and twists of the trail inclines. About halfway, a distant sound brought him to a halt.

CHAPTER TWENTY-THREE

THE FOOTSTEP WAS BIG. Not the delicate hop of a chipmunk foraging past their bedtime. Something with weight. A monstrous crunch of branches and leaves that sat undisturbed on the forest floor.

Casper's fingertips moistened. Throat dried up. Muscles tensed. Goosebumps spread across his forearms despite the warm autumn temperature. Such a strange phenomenon. Goosebumps. For some reason, it made him think of Gil.

If Delaney's source was right, Gil was inside the park. Somewhere. He could be hunting for evidence too. On his own. *Oh, no. Gil.*

He could stumble into their trap. Casper considered his options. He racked his brain for a way to communicate in the thick darkness of nighttime. A way to let the team know it could be Zoe's fiancé romping around with his lab coat on. Not Bigfoot. *How the hell did I not think of this sooner? Gil.*

Casper saw Zoe sit up straight from her post but saw no movement from Delaney. His heart thumped in his chest like a kick drum. It pulsed in his ears. Anticipation soaked through his skin.

Sweat beaded on his brow. A wave of his arms got Zoe's attention, but she just nodded and pointed towards the sound. Casper cupped his ear in that direction.

CRUNCH. Another step. Followed by another. Something was walking. Two feet. *What was the term Gil used? Bi-pedal?* Two feet. Like a human. *CRUNCH.* The creature was getting closer. Walking towards them. An owl hooted in a far-off tree. Casper took it as a warning. His heart rate skyrocketed. He forced himself to breathe, but the breaths were shallow. Guarded. Anticipatory.

Casper counted each step. After the tenth, the movement stopped. It had sounded close. Within a few yards. Spitting distance. He waited for an eleventh. Nothing came. From his vantage point, there was no visual evidence yet. Nothing that would spark action. They needed the beast to make a move. A shadow flickered off to his left. He figured Delaney was shuffling in her post, gripping her pistol and getting into position. He saw no movement from Zoe's corner.

Casper glanced back toward his left and saw the flicker again. It wasn't Delaney. It was something else. Something big. *Breathe. Breathe. Inhale. Exhale. Inhale. Exhale. Inhale.*

Another step. This one was closer. Now it was moving faster. Running. Running towards them. The shape towered in the shadows, but it was too dark to make out anything besides its outline. Behind the figure, Casper saw another silhouette. Delaney was in position. *Wait, is that Delaney?*

The beast stepped with care. Lifting each leg like an infant still learning how to walk as he sprinted. Clumsy and uncomfortable. The clamorous snap of twigs beneath its feet was the only sound echoing through the forest canopies. Casper held his breath and willed the beast to come a few feet closer. Just another yard. It took another step. It was so close now. Whatever it was, it paused and looked around, craning its neck with hesitation.

"FREEZE!" Zoe's voice boomed from the north. The creature shot a look in that direction and froze before finding its bearings and taking off like a bullet from a gun. The creature sprinted out of the clearing. Leaves thrashed in its wake. Casper steadied his arm but lowered his pepper spray as the creature sped away.

He watched the beast pass through a thicket of trees. A silhouette dove out of the shadows and speared the creature to the ground.

CHAPTER TWENTY-FOUR

THE SOUND DIDN'T RETURN. Andy pushed on. His breath clouded in front of him like when he let out a puff of cigarette smoke. His body craved it. Anything. Something to numb the sensation of reality. With each mile that he covered, he cursed himself for not quitting that junk years ago. Swearing it all off. Going straight and sober. The phone lit his way through the abandoned trails and within minutes, the path beneath his feet changed from gravel to concrete. He was on a road.

A lack of signage and miles of split-post fencing mirrored every other stretch of park interior he'd seen to date. The park's system of roads led to different parking lots and structures around the land, some of which Andy had navigated during daylight hour trips with Ava and Andrew. The location flashed on the screen and he tiptoed towards it. There was no sound besides his breath and the pitter-patter of his feet on the pavement. He looked up. A starless night. He tried to decide if that was good luck or bad but before he could land on a decision, the phone zoomed in. He was close.

Sirens blared. The noise was sudden and foreign in such a thick forest. Even the oaks and yellow poplars stood still in the night sky. The sound grew louder but remained at a distance. Andy breathed easy.

A far-off light flickered between the trees, and Andy dove to the side of the road. When nothing followed, he got back to his feet, wiped the dirt from his pants, and checked the signal again. It was directing him towards the light. Andy squinted in the inky night sky to determine if the structure in the distance was a house, a shack, or some sort of trap set by the local police. He crept closer.

His breath was louder now. Like a cricket in the quiet of a summer night. In and out. He poked his head around the trunk and could see better. It was a house. A small one. Off in the distance. The light was coming from the kitchen where there appeared to be people milling about. Chatting and laughing like a tailgate outside of a football game. Andy cursed under his breath. He pressed on.

He stayed within the cover of the trees and approached step by step. He rounded the entire house without crossing into view of the window where he'd seen people inside. The map zoomed in again. The beacon flashed in the backyard. He ducked behind a stack of chopped wood and caught his breath. The air felt icy in his lungs. He unzipped the bag, reached inside and pulled out the contents. Under the faint light from his phone screen, he glanced at them. *What the hell?*

Andy thought back to the second message. *'Leave the contents out. Hide it in plain view.'* He took a breath and lifted a log from the top of the woodpile. He dropped the backpack's contents underneath, and the log fell back into place without a sound. Andy let out a deep exhale and crawled back into the thick forest behind him. A door swung open as he stepped into the darkness, and he crouched down behind a thick stump ten yards into the brush. He looked up at the person who stepped out of the house.

The person wore a tan uniform with green pants. A badge

reflected under the overhead light and looked bronze. *Police?* He pushed himself into a ball and willed himself to get smaller. Smaller. The light shut off; the door clanked shut and voices started back up inside the house. Andy waited twenty long minutes until the coast was clear. Then he made the long trek back to his car. All the while, he fought with his inner demons and asked himself repeatedly.

Why would The Fox send me to a cop's house?

CHAPTER TWENTY-FIVE

CASPER SPRINTED OVER. His feet moved like a dancer that knew every step. He hurdled root beds and fallen branches. The rotting trunk of a downed oak was his biggest hurdle, but he was up and over it like a gymnast. The thrash of Delaney hurrying his way sounded as she sprinted. An explosion of sounds and movement in the calm of the dusky woods. From the corner of his eye, he couldn't see Zoe. Casper figured she had to be the shadow that took out the beast. *But it was the wrong direction. What the hell was that?*

He closed in on the scene and stared at the ground. Out of breath, he stood with his hands on his knees and surveyed the forest floor. His eyes grew wide as he took in the hulking mass below. Limbs laid motionless. Zoe caught up and paused next to him. The group gasped for breath like runners at the end of a half marathon. Nobody took their eyes off the beast on the ground.

Beneath them, a tall creature in a furry costume lay face down on the soil. At first motionless, it now began moaning in agony, holding its arm and wailing. The cry was human. Distinctly human. Casper's goosebumps faded away as he took his eyes off the creature and looked at the shadowy figure who had taken it down. Gil.

Gil winced and held his ribs as he rolled around in the dirt. His left arm hung low. Zoe hurried to him. She held her hand on his face. "What the hell, Gil? I thought it was you in the suit!"

"I'm sorry, I'm—" Gil nodded towards the creature's body. "Go. Tell me what it is."

Zoe joined Casper and Delaney, who were standing over the large, hairy figure that was motionless on the ground. Casper watched as Delaney's eyes registered the scene before her and her jaw fall open. He shook his head and furrowed his brow. "I'll call the police."

"Hold on, I told Russo we'd call her first," Zoe said and reached for her phone.

She stepped into the clearing. Casper and Delaney met eyes and shook their heads. Delaney grinned. "Some vacation, huh?"

Nobody else spoke until Zoe returned. The creature on the ground wailed in agony, but nobody paid him any mind. "They have a unit stationed down the road so they'll be here within minutes. They can meet us at the gate."

"What about animal control?" Gil asked from the side.

"No reason to call them," Zoe said and kicked at the beast's long, skinny legs. The human inside wailed louder.

"Well, we can eliminate one option at least," Casper said.

Gil's pained voice whispered from the ground. "Is it... is it... somebody take a photo. We'll need proof. Evidence. We—"

"Gil, we won't need evidence of squat," Delaney said.

"It's human, Gil. It's somebody in a Bigfoot costume," Zoe said with a sigh.

"A rather large someone..." Casper said.

"Is it alive?" Gil asked.

"Seems to be," Casper said. "Zoe?"

"Yeah?"

"I believe this is the moment where you pull off the mask."

"You can do the honors. I'm afraid my temper will lead to our second assault in the park if I get too close."

Casper edged towards the body with one hand on the borrowed pepper spray in his pocket. Zoe held her breath. Delaney did the same. Gil propped himself up on his elbows but fell back to the ground with a thump that echoed through the tree trunks. Zoe helped him up with one hand. He stood hunched over, still panting, with his eyes fixed on Casper.

In one swift movement, Casper tugged the creature's mask off and tossed it to the side. Zoe's eyes grew wide. Nobody spoke a word. They just stared.

CHAPTER TWENTY-SIX

As THE FLASHING lights of the police cruisers faded into the dark, Casper and Gil stared up at the pink sky signaling the approach of a new day. Delaney jogged over toward them and nodded.

"Gil. One quick question," Casper said.

"I would anticipate that you have significantly more than one question but please, proceed."

"I'll leave the full interrogation to your fiancé. For now, I'd just like to ask about your past. Did you play football in high school?"

Gil laughed. "Do I appear as if I played football in high school?"

"No, but I wanted to make sure. If there's a coach out there teaching that type of god-awful tackling technique, I'd like to wring his neck before the end of the week," Casper said.

Delaney chuckled. "I could barely see it from where I was. You were invisible out there."

"Yeah, about that. How did you know where we'd be?" Casper asked.

"Despite your frequency in the environment, you Park Rangers are not so stealth in the woods. You travel like a herd of elephants in a mud field. I have tracked many creatures in past research. It was not remotely challenging to identify your path and follow behind while keeping a distance."

"But why not just come join us?" Delaney asked with her arms crossed.

"To be blunt, I was scared that Zoe would yell so loud that the, er, visitor would be scared off. Or perhaps she would cause an avalanche in a far-off mountain. Regardless, I did not enjoy the thought of dealing with my enraged fiancé. A coward's approach, I am aware."

Delaney nodded. "Her bad side is not someplace I'd reckon anybody wants to be."

The roar of an approaching truck caught everybody's attention. Mathias stormed out of his driver's seat like his feet were on fire. He stood in front of the group, one hand on his hip with the other tugging on his mustache. "Where's Watts?"

Casper stepped forward. "She went with Detective Russo back to the station."

Mathias turned to Gil. "Gilbert. I know what you did."

Gil gulped and looked at the ground. Mathias chuckled. "Looks like we have a much bigger problem on our hand. What can you all tell me?"

"It was a human in a Bigfoot costume. He said nothing to us. Just cried from Gil's tackle."

Mathias eyed Gil. "And to think, they all just thought you were this slouch of a researcher living like a leech off Zoe's teat."

"Hey now," Delaney interrupted. "Enough of that. That won't help anybody clean up this mess."

Mathias grinned, let go of his mustache, and stormed away from the group. Casper expected to see a dust cloud gather behind his tires as he sped off, but it was just a thunderous roar of an engine that faded into the night. Gil looked at the others. "Would you like a ride back home? Perhaps we could all shower and wash ourselves of this evening's events."

After a silent, bumpy walk to the car, Gil drove them to the cottage. He let Casper and Delaney into the house and they were greeted by a joyous Hoagie. He made his rounds and rolled onto his back to receive belly rubs from all, Gil included. Once they settled him down, they plopped themselves onto the couch. While they each showered, Gil made coffee, which tasted like battery acid to Casper, but he needed the caffeine more than anything. Delaney made herself tea to avoid the abhorrent liquid.

"So, Gil. Where'd you go?" Delaney said.

Gil sighed. "When I first left, I thought that if I gave Zoe some space, she would comprehend that I meant no harm. That thought soon washed away. She is stubborn, as you well know. Like a wolverine or a mule. I remembered I had a tent in my trunk and decided that the best course of action was to prove my case by solving the mystery. Thus, I re-entered the wilderness with a new mission and spirit."

"Which mystery is this?"

"I am not a criminology expert, so I did not see how I could assist with the Wade Buchanon assault. That is better left for experts in the field. Further, I did not see how it was all connected. I remain unable to tie one event to the other. But I know creatures. I believe deep down I expected that these sightings were a hoax. I just did not want to admit it to myself or my book editor and—"

"Yeah, we saw the note from him."

Gil stood and began pacing around the room. "It is, as Zoe would say, *messed up*. But it overjoyed part of me to have new experiences to put into the book. It was a natural second season of the podcast. I was off and running with a reinvigorated inspiration that had evaporated long ago."

"What made you come around then?" Casper asked and set down his mug on the table. No amount of energy was worth drinking the tart excuse for coffee.

"At some point, sitting in the woods, I took off my metaphorical Bigfoot expert hat and put on my metaphorical lab coat. I started from the beginning and looked at the evidence without the bias that I had insisted to Zoe that I did not have."

"Smart move. What took you so long?" Delaney asked with her arms crossed.

"Hope blinded me. There is a certain mockery that people like me, people that follow urban legends and lore around, get around town. I thought that maybe..." His voice drifted off as he stared into his mug.

"Maybe you'd be proven right?"

"Yeah. It is stupid."

"Not stupid at all, Gil. Nobody wants to be called the village idiot. So, when you looked at the evidence as a scientist, what was your hypothesis?"

"The likely scenario is that somebody hoped to cause a scene. This was intentional. A byproduct of something else. Not some magical moment where an urban legend came to life. Just a fool trying to play a trick on people."

"Sure looks that way," Delaney said. She reached for her phone as it vibrated and excused herself to the other room. Hoagie followed her with a toy ball in his mouth.

"Casper?"

"Yeah, Gil?"

"What do I do now?"

"I think—" Casper stopped when Delaney reentered the room.

"That was Zoe. She'd like Casper and me to come down to the station and watch the interview of our furry friend." Hoagie let out a bark. Delaney knelt down to him. "A different furry friend, Hoagie."

Gil nodded. "Glad that she is keeping you two informed. Let me know how I can help. I should bathe and begin writing my apologies."

Casper went into the bathroom and washed his face. The grime from a long night in the woods had speckled dirt on his cheeks that fell into the sink after a hearty scrub. The earthy smell on his hands gave way, replaced by the hibiscus and lavender soap's aroma. Within minutes, Casper had washed away the night's mayhem. It weighed his body down toward the earth with a distinct tiredness that came from a sleepless night. After a change of clothes, he met Delaney back in the living room.

"Ready?"

"Let's go for it," Casper added. "You alright?"

Delaney grinned. "I'm the one that is trained for this life. I should ask you that. How are you holding up?"

"It's all a bit confusing and freaky. But the skeptic in me is happy to see a human face behind it all."

"Fair enough." Delaney moved in closer to him. "And thank you for not mentioning Raven Rock like I asked. I promise, we'll clear the air down the road."

He nodded and kissed her on the cheek. She slid the car keys into his hand. "I'll meet you out there in a second. Just want to check on Gil."

Casper stepped out. The floor creaked as Delaney walked towards Gil's bedroom, where she found him sitting with his head in his hands.

"Hey, Gil?"

He looked up, red with embarrassment. "Yes, Delaney?"

"Zoe and I are cut from the same cloth. We grew up in different homes, but both took the same path. Both tough on the outside, but big old softies inside. Both took up careers in law enforcement, although she opted to patrol the trails over the streets. Anyway, all that to say, I know her. Be upfront. Be honest. Be yourself and she will forgive you for anything."

Gil nodded. "Thank you, Delaney. I mean it."

"One more thing. Why don't you come with us down to the station?"

"You believe that is a wise move?"

"This puzzle requires all hands on deck. I think Zoe would appreciate it. We'll wait for you in the driveway."

Gil smiled, and Delaney left to meet Casper in the car.

Casper let the car run to blast warm air into the tiny space. Delaney hopped in.

"Gil is coming, so hold on a minute."

Casper nodded. "Okay, but one favor?"

"What's up?"

"Can you be the one to explain to him why we need to stop and find some drinkable coffee on the way over?"

CHAPTER TWENTY-SEVEN

"DYLAN MCQUEENEY. TWENTY-FOUR YEARS OLD." Russo nodded towards the window that looked into the interrogation room where McQueeney sat. "Just a kid. Family lives over in Durham off Redding Lane. He's agreed to talk to us so long as we consider *a deal*," she said with a grin.

Zoe glanced at him. "A deal? For what?"

"I don't know." Russo laughed. "These people see a lot of TV and they think the police traffic information for 'get out of jail free' cards. Either way, he's agreed to open up."

"Mind if I sit in?"

"I was going to insist if you didn't ask yourself." Russo turned towards the door, then stopped. "Another thing you should know. We pulled a sample of the fur on his costume and sent it over to our forensics team. Luckily, somebody was pulling an all-nighter and agreed to help. At first glance, they're reporting that the fibers are different. That doesn't hurt our case against Mr. McQueeney but it leaves the door open for other explanations."

Zoe nodded. Russo held the door open. "Follow me, Zoe."

The two women entered the cramped interrogation room and

McQueeney looked up from his chair. He smiled at them but wiped it away. Zoe watched the rhythmic tapping of his left leg on the ground. Russo was right, this guy was just a boy trapped in a man's body.

"Thank you for speaking with us, Dylan," Russo said.

McQueeney nodded. "I—uh. How can I help?"

"Well, maybe start with a brief explanation of why you were parading around the woods in an oversized gorilla suit that appears custom made for you."

"You know, I always wondered if I was breaking the law." He chuckled to himself. "Now, I see it. Clear as day. Look, I don't want to go to jail. I'll say anything you want."

"Well, Dylan, we've got a man in the hospital and all signs are pointing to you being the man who put him there."

McQueeney's eyes grew wide. "What? No. No. Nothing like that. Hell no. I've never hurt anybody. Except for my little brother. Greg. He's a pest, though. Always borrowing clothes and—"

"Why were you in the suit, Dylan?" Russo prodded.

"It's… well… it's a long story."

"We've got all day."

"I'll keep it short. I swear to you, this is the truth. I was part of a group on Reddit. You know, the online network? Well, I had joined this RTP-Part-Time Jobs group to find some ways to make some extra cash on the side. I dropped out of Duke last year and needed to find enough dough to get back in. Anyway, I posted about myself and somebody messaged me directly."

"And?"

"And they asked me two questions. The first was *can you keep a secret?*. That didn't throw me off. Maybe it should have. The internet is a super weird place. Reddit especially. I mean, I was hoping it wasn't somehow a sexual fetish or something but… like, I didn't want to go and take pictures of girl's feet or something but—"

"What was the second question, Dylan?"

"Oh. They asked me how tall I was."

"And you are?"

"Six foot five."

"And then what happened?"

"They asked my address. I gave it. I was desperate. They said it was a down payment. It was... a lot of cash. Then they told me they'd follow up with a package and instructions. So, I get this package. I open it up and here's this costume. Like a Sasquatch or something. Anyway, the instructions were simple. They told me to walk through the park before it opens. Like around sunrise."

"That's it?"

"They said to stay off the trails and to avoid being seen as often as I could. And that if I got spotted, I should run like the wind."

Russo glanced at Zoe with a confused look on her face. "When did this all start?"

"Six months ago."

"And do you have any proof this story is legitimate?" Zoe asked.

"I took screenshots of the entire conversation on my computer and took photos of the instructions and all. I knew something funky was going on here. It just felt wrong. But the money felt right." He looked at his hands cuffed to the table. "Did I do something illegal? How long will I be in prison, Detective?"

"If your story checks out, you will be free to go in a matter of moments. I just have one last question before I let my colleague, Ranger Watts here, take over the rest of the questioning. She's in charge of that lovely park you were stomping around in."

"I'm so sorry, I'm—"

"Where were you around dawn on Saturday morning?"

"Saturday? I slept in."

"Can anybody verify that for us?"

"No, I mean, I was alone. I'm single right now. Those dating apps, man, they're brutal. It's like a needle in an ugly, boring haystack. Plus, I love rollerblading. Why should I hide that? I swear—"

"So, you have no alibi? Nobody who can verify your story?" Russo pressed on.

"I don't have an alibi because I didn't do anything wrong."

Russo nodded. "We'll have to look into that. Ranger Watts will take over now." She winked and whispered. "Be gentle, Zoe."

Zoe cleared her throat and tried to process all the information that had Dylan McQueeney had spewed out. She dismissed her initial questions but settled on a point that had continued to bug her. "Did you intentionally trigger a game camera in the woods on Friday night?"

"Yes."

"How did you know it was there, Dylan?"

McQueeney let out a deep sigh. "Okay, I left out one thing. Will that add time to my sentence? Can I at least go to a prison nearby so my family can visit? Oh, God, I hope they visit. But that will wreck my mom. She's so fragile and—"

"Dylan. What did you leave out?"

"I would get emails. With information."

"Like what?"

"Like when you rangers were off duty. When the campground was empty. Any road closures. And Friday afternoon, I got a message telling me to look for a camera on a tree near the lake."

"And you found the camera? Why didn't you avoid it?"

"Avoid it? I did what the email told me to do. Toss a rock and run away from it. I don't know how those things work. I thought that broke it or something. Wait, is that how you found me? Gosh darn it, I—"

Zoe turned to Russo and whispered. "The only people that knew about that camera were the rangers."

Russo nodded towards the door, and they left together. In the hallway, they discussed the interrogation of the costumed fool in whispered tones.

"The rangers could have told somebody, though. Family or friends."

"Maybe, but that's a weird piece of information to share that quickly. Friday afternoon is right around the time that the cameras were being set up."

"Who set them up, Zoe?"

"Clem and Ernest. The other rangers in the park. Could be one of them."

"Look, since Bozo the clown in there isn't looking guilty for the assault on Wade Buchanon, I'm inclined to send everybody home to get some rest. It's an ungodly hour already."

Zoe stared at her feet. Russo punched her lightly in the shoulder.

"Hell of a bust, Ranger Watts. You found your Bigfoot. Now, let's see if we can trace this back to Wade Buchanon somehow. Call me after you get some sleep. And Zoe?"

"Yeah?"

"Tread lightly with your co-workers. Don't want to go burning any bridges over an idiot like Dylan McQueeney."

Zoe grinned and met Casper and Delaney in the observation room. Delaney hugged her. "You alright? That was some heavy frowning you were doing in there, Zo."

"I spent half of the time trying to think of what the hell was going on and the other half trying to think of how I'd make it up to Gil."

"No need. He's the one who owes you big," Gil said as he emerged from the waiting room. He smiled and kissed Zoe.

"Gil, I—"

"You don't have to say a word. I have a whole suitcase of sorries waiting for you when we can wrap this thing up. But in the meantime, I'm here and I've got your back unequivocally."

Tears welled up in Zoe's eyes. She wiped them away and nodded at him. "Anybody got any ideas?"

"This case just got a lot more complicated. But I think I have a grasp on it," Casper said.

"Spill the beans, champ. I'm all ears," Zoe added.

"Well, this is a weird question, but... have any of you ever learned a magic trick?"

Delaney kicked him in the shin. "This is no time for jokes, Casper Kelly!"

"No jokes! I'm serious. When I was a kid, my dad took me to this magic shop where each year for my birthday, they would teach me a new trick. I grew out of the whole thing by the time I was a teenager, but some of the basics still stuck with me."

"And you're about to pull a deck of cards out of your pocket? Come on, Casper. Time is wasting," Delaney said.

"In a well-executed card trick, for example, the key is to make the audience look where you want them to. If you're doing something clever with the cards with your right hand, you want them to look at your left while you do it."

"A diversion," Zoe said.

"Exactly. What better diversion than a sudden uptick in Bigfoot sightings that demand the full attention of the entire park staff?"

"But a diversion from what?" Gil asked.

"That's the key. If you find that answer, you can unlock everything."

"Okay, so where do we go with that information? We know somebody was possibly trying to avert our attention with this whole charade. And that it worked," said Zoe.

"And we know they had an inside man," Delaney added.

"I'm willing to wager that whoever that inside man is may also be the holder of the key to unraveling this entire mystery."

"Well, let's track him down!" Zoe said and waved for the crowd to follow.

CHAPTER TWENTY-EIGHT

CIGARETTE SMOKE CREPT out of the cracked window next to Andy in his beat-up old Civic. Butts sat in a tray of ashes that were overflowing into the cupholder. He reached for another before the one in his mouth ended. In front of him, uniformed officers rushed in and out of the station. He gripped the flask stashed beneath his thigh and snuck a sip once he was alone. The uniforms were different than that of the man he'd seen the night before. Still, there were similarities. Men and women of the law. Each one strode by without so much as a glance in Andy's direction, but his heart rate soared each time that he saw their badges reflect in the hazy sunlight of the day.

He unlocked his phone and pulled up his thread with Kyle. Still nothing. His partner-in-crime had been silent since he left the soccer field on Sunday morning. A substitute teacher had to be pulled in at the last minute when nobody heard from him before the morning bell. The school administration cursed Kyle's name. Andy was just worried. In a twisted way, he felt responsible, even though Kyle had gotten them into this mess in the first place.

An hour earlier, Andy navigated the maze of condominiums

in the small lake community in Cary that Kyle called home. Three times. Three times Andy had walked the Cedar Pointe Condominium loop that was bracketed by identical buildings with white siding and dark green shutters. Windows in the same spots. Like somebody hit copy and paste a few too many times.

On the second pass, he caught his first break. Kyle's car. The hope was short-lived. His car was in a guest spot. One of the few without a number that would have been a helpful hint as to which of the identical units he called home. *He may have parked there to avoid detection. To stay anonymous. But at least it means he didn't drive off.*

Three additional calls to Kyle's phone yielded nothing but his cold voicemail message. *Kyle Pittman. Leave a message.* The tone sounded harsher each time.

He had wandered the sidewalk near the car, hoping to find a neighbor kind enough to answer Andy's questions. But everybody that he saw was approaching retirement. He had little hope but was growing desperate.

Andy approached an elderly couple walking their Scottish Terrier. "Hi, excuse me?" The tiny ferocious beast snarled at him as he approached.

"Can I help you, young man?" The husband asked. He hushed the dog, whose snarl had turned into tiny cartoonish yelps.

"I hope so. I'm looking for my friend, Kyle. Kyle Pittman. Young man with brown hair and a short beard. About my height. Runs a lot. He lives somewhere in Cedar Pointe but I can't remember which unit he was in."

"Does he face the lake or the street?" The woman asked with a frown.

"I don't know, I'm sorry."

"Well, if you were his friend you would at least know that much. We can't go about helping strangers," she barked back. It reminded Andy a lot of the tiny Scottish Terrier next to her.

"We work together and he didn't show up today. So, I wanted to check on him. Just make sure everything is okay, you know?"

Something in the air rubbed the woman the wrong way. Her face shifted into a scowl. "I don't know the name." She crossed her arms and nodded towards the parking lot. "Which car is his? Sometimes we know people by their cars."

"Smart thinking, Margaret," the husband added.

"Hush John, he's talking."

Andy pointed towards Kyle's SUV. "The navy blue one there."

"Oh, he's one of those folks that are driving in and out of the lot at all hours of the night." Margaret sighed. "His headlights flicker through our windows when we try to sleep. We're on the ground floor in the 700 block. We've tried blackout curtains, but the lights at night still make their way into our bedroom!"

"I'm sorry. He works two jobs. I know—"

"I don't know which unit is his. I'm sorry we couldn't be more helpful," John said and ushered Margaret away before she could shout at Andy again. *Some luck.*

Andy's mind continued to race under the influence of nicotine and over-sugared energy drinks. *He's dead. The Fox killed him. And I'm next.* Andy checked his watch and pulled out of the police station lot. He drove under the speed limit the rest of the way until an idea popped into his head. Then he pressed the gas.

Back at Pine Hills High, Andy popped in an old VHS tape from the History Channel and stepped out of the classroom. He jogged down the hall and smiled at the secretary. Andy had never cracked the icy exterior that protected Jessica Arwood from the world. Somehow, despite his irresistible charm, Jessica appeared immune. She often smelled of cigarettes, much like Andy, but he'd never seen her in the reserved smoking section for staff.

He wound up his biggest smile as he approached the desk. "Jessica! How are you? That's a lovely blouse you have there—"

"What do you want, Andy?"

"Can't a man compliment a woman without—"

"What. Do. You. Want," the ice queen barked. Jessica seemed a lot like the Scottish Terrier from the parking lot.

"Okay, geez. I heard that Kyle Pittman was out today. No call in with plans for the sub either." Andy smiled. "We're friends and that doesn't seem like him, so I was hoping to check on him after I'm done with practice."

Jessica glared at him and crossed her arms. "Okay, go ahead. I don't see why this needs to involve me."

"Well, you see, Jessica..." Andy leaned up against the counter. "The thing is that I don't remember which unit he lives in over at Cedar Pointe. I was there once to watch football, but that was last year. They all look the same."

"You want his address?" She raised her eyebrows.

"Yeah, is that possible?"

"It's no secret among the staff. There's a directory that you get at the beginning of the year with everybody's cell and address." She looked him over and sighed again. "I'm going to guess you never took the time to read through it. Probably collecting dust on a shelf somewhere."

"I've never needed—"

"No, I get it. Let me pull the address for you since we cannot trouble you to keep track of your things." Jessica's voice dripped with sarcasm.

Andy forced a smile so hard his cheeks hurt. "Thanks so much, Jessica. You're a lifesaver. Now I see why everybody raves about how great you are at your job."

She waved him off. "Enough of that B.S. Looks like he's at 712 Winterspoon Drive. That enough for you or would you like me to chauffeur you to his front door in a stretch limo too?"

Andy entered the address into his phone and saw that each unit had its own address. "Bingo. Thanks so much!"

"Yeah, and if you see him, tell him I will personally kick his ass if he disappears like this again," Jessica shouted like a disappointed mother. "We're all adults here. Just say you're sick if you're sick. He's better off dead at this point."

Andy gulped but ignored the ironic choice of words. He grinned and Jessica mumbled under her breath.

"Wiseass. Thinking he can outfox the system by not logging his sick days in the portal. You tell him!" Jessica's voice rose to a shout. "I don't care if he's too hungover or—"

"Yeah, thanks, Jessica! Will do," Andy said.

As he turned to go, Jessica whispered to him. "Also, grab yourself some gum before you drive anywhere. Not that it's any of my business..."

Andy nodded. His cheeks flushed red, and he excused himself back to his classroom. The next few hours would drag on like the dull second act of Ava's middle school presentation of *Guys and Dolls*. Anticipation and fear coursed through his veins. He had big plans for the evening.

CHAPTER TWENTY-NINE

BETWEEN HALF-EMPTY COFFEE mugs and glasses of water, an officer laid out every email exchange between Dylan McQueeney and his source. Each message was brief, bordering on abrupt. Russo had sent the correspondence off to an electronic forensics team but warned that they move at a snail's pace.

A three-hour nap had done more harm than good, and Casper's eyelids were heavy as anvils. Between sips of coffee, he studied each thread of the case with great detail. He paused over every word, often rereading a sentence or two. Delaney followed close behind but took frequent breaks to check in on Zoe's morale. The early reports were concerning, but things had taken a recent uptick.

"I'm alright, I swear, Laney," Zoe promised. "It's like a bomb just dropped on the park, but it's not anything criminal yet. It's just... weird."

"We can handle these files if you want to go take a walk or take—"

"Laney, I'm in this. Hell, I think I'm closer to an answer than I ever was."

"If you insist. Casper, you find anything yet?"

Casper jogged around the backside of the large oak table, grabbed one piece of paper from the pile, and handed it over to Zoe and Delaney.

"What am I looking at here?" Delaney asked.

"It's a shift schedule of sorts. It has circles on certain nights of the week, but something is blocking the names of who is working when. Do you recognize this at all, Zoe?"

"Yeah, this is our shift schedule Mathias puts together. We have to submit things like PTO and all that, so there's coverage at all times. The yellow highlight means that the ranger in that row is on call for the night."

"What does that entail? Like a security detail?" Casper asked.

"It just means that if somebody has an issue or something out of the ordinary happens, that ranger is the person to get called. We trade off a little old flip Nokia phone that rings louder than a church bell when somebody calls. If you ever want to see Gil shiver, play that ringtone for him."

"And if somebody calls, what then?"

"Often it's somebody in the campground who missed the gate and needs to be let in. On the weekends it may be rowdiness or some kids sneaking around the park at night, but that's rare. It's just a plan for emergencies."

"But if somebody saw something odd in the early hours?"

"They'd call the on-call number and whoever was responsible would have to get up and check it out. I only had one call about the sightings during my shifts. I think Clem had two. Maybe Ernest had one of them, I honestly forget."

"Was there always a call?"

"No, it all depends on timing and who was around. So, I'd imagine that on more than one occasion something was seen but not reported. Or just not seen at all. People turn a blind eye to things when they're still wiping the sleep out of their eyes, you know?"

"And eyewitness testimony is flawed, to say the least," Delaney added.

"Can we track down the original copy of this to compare? I'd guess it's this year. The month has thirty days so that would only leave April, June, and September since November is next month."

Zoe glanced at the sheet. "I'd be willing to guess it's September. There's a pink highlight over Monday the 7th. That's Labor Day. I'll ask Joanne to pull it from our records."

Zoe stepped out of the room and left Casper and Delaney alone. Casper stared at the paper to discern a clue. Delaney nudged him with her shoulder.

"What?" he said with a grin.

"You're cute when you're focused."

"Behave yourself, Shepard. We've got a case to solve," Casper whispered.

"What if I don't want to beha—"

Zoe walked back into the room. "That was some painful flirting, Laney. What are you, in middle school? *'You're cute when you're focused.'*"

"Shut up. I can still beat you up, you know."

"Threatening an officer? You're lucky I've got bigger fish to fry, ma'am," Zoe laughed.

"Hate to break up a family squabble, but why did you suspect Clem right away?"

"Gut instinct, I guess."

"Are you sure? Nothing more than that?"

"I mean, he's detestable as a man, but I've gotten over that. The armchair psychologist in me has diagnosed him with severe insecurity around powerful women."

"And he was first on the scene."

"Yeah, I considered that too. But to be honest, he looked panicked. Not the panic that occurs when you've just screwed up. But the panic where he just didn't know what to do. Plus, I could see his hands. Unless he had a weapon that was tossed into the lake, his hands were spotless."

"He had a fishing pole, right?"

"Yeah, but Detective Russo said that the wounds appeared to be hand-to-hand combat. She also mentioned that Wade Buchanon had no defensive wounds. The forensics team suspects the attacker took him by surprise. He never stood a chance."

"Jesus."

"But I do have some good news. As I was leaving the station Russo mentioned that Buchanon seems to be turning the corner. They're keeping the case marked as an assault with some guarded optimism."

"Tough situation for a detective to be in. Stakes get a lot higher when it's murder, but nobody wants that," Delaney added. "If I may say so myself. I am, in my other life, a detective, after all."

"You don't say? You have failed to mention that in the entire three days that you've been here. That must be a record. You see, Casper, Delaney here was playing detective when she was a little kid. Her mom had given her a little play badge, and she'd run around interrogating kids in the neighborhood over the smallest things. What was your biggest case back then, Nancy Drew?"

"We had a lot of suspects in the missing ice cream incident of '94."

"And what was the verdict?"

"Jury is still out. Curious you'd bring that up after all these years, Laney. Guilty conscious?"

Joanne knocked on the conference room door and handed Zoe a file. "Here's what you asked for. I had to print it out since most of the timesheets are digital these days. I don't see why you needed the shift schedule though."

"Thanks, Joanne. We're exhausting all of our options here," Zoe replied.

"But I thought you caught the man last night? It was all that anybody wanted to talk about this morning before you came in. Even Mathias cracked a smile."

"We're still piecing this together. I may need additional information, so I'll buzz you if I do. That okay?"

"Sure is! Ooh! This feels just like one of those special episodes of *CSI*. Or *Criminal Minds*. I've always preferred *Criminal Minds*. Shemar Moore is a dreamboat. Phew. Okay, I'll be alone upfront thinking of Shemar. Good luck, Zoe!"

Zoe placed the shift schedule next to the redacted one from McQueeney. When they matched up, the names labeled who had each shift. A handful of circles were on the page.

"What did the circles represent again?"

"McQueeney said they are the times he was told to head into the park and cause a scene from a distance."

"Huh," Delaney said.

"What's up?"

"Well, maybe it's the Nancy Drew in me, but something is suspicious here."

"How do you mean?"

"Well, all the rows have circles except for one."

"So, everybody but one ranger appears scheduled for the bullshit. Looks like somebody didn't want to be jumping out of bed in the middle of the night."

Zoe furrowed her brow and kicked the chair in front of her. She hollered for Mathias to join them in the conference room. He instead called for her to step into his office. She glanced back into the room before she departed. "If I still have a job after this conversation, we're going after Ernest Henley with everything we've got."

CHAPTER THIRTY

MATHIAS GLARED with such intensity that Zoe thought he may bore a hole through the wall. He tugged at his mustache with unusual ferocity and opened his mouth but no words escaped. She took the lead instead.

"Mathias, I know that I—"

He raised a hand. "Did I ever tell you about my first week on the job here?"

Zoe shook her head. "I'm not even sure when you got here."

"It was early 2001. I came in as a Ranger 1. Eager to make a difference. Spend some time in nature. I was a lot like you are today."

"Not sure if that's a compliment or-"

"On my third day, a tropical storm came in and crushed the region. It came with an intensity that the meteorologists didn't predict, so things took a turn. We had a massive oak take a fall right over the main road between the parking lot and the exit. Cars were backed up, trying to evacuate, but the trunk blocked their path. I rushed into action. I was in there, knee-deep in the puddles from overflowing culverts. The other rangers were all there too. But they were calmer. Stoic, almost."

Zoe nodded. "As if they'd been there before."

"Exactly. Within a half-hour, I had run out of gas. The other rangers had stepped in with chainsaws and moved swiftly. Before long, I was on the sidelines. Watching. No better than anybody sitting in their cozy car waiting for relief."

"I get it," Zoe said with a grin. "You gained a reverence for experience. It's why you respect Ernest so much and—"

"More or less. But I also learned that there's an order to the park. An intentional structure to how we make decisions and handle unusual circumstances. When that tree fell, I was acting like I was in it alone. I was not. I was part of a team that had my best interests in mind. But I failed them."

Zoe nodded. "And I failed you."

Mathias sighed. "You did and you didn't. When I heard about your little sting operation in the woods, I boiled with rage. But I was even angrier that you got results."

"But we needed answers. We needed—"

"You needed to respect my orders and stay out of it. But you didn't. I thought I saw potential in you. A future Superintendent. But you found those answers you were searching for, anyway. So, the lesson you learned was not that you should have listened but that you can skirt around the rules and it'll work out. I doubt that will take you very far."

"Sir, I don't think that's the case. I don't know why this got ahold of me but I—"

"Save it. We can discuss your future when this all wraps up. But for now, you've opened Pandora's box. We'll have to reckon with what follows." He stood and dropped his hands to his side. "What did you all find in there, anyway?"

Mathias analyzed the papers with the same care a retiree reserved for their crossword puzzle. Each detail counted.

Each box filled correctly. Zoe paced across the room. The facts didn't add up. Ernest could be a jerk, but he was no criminal.

Zoe's patience wore thin as she watched him take in the evidence. "What do you think?"

"It's compelling."

"What do we do now?" Zoe said. "Where is Ernest today?"

Mathias glanced at his phone and then looked up. "Home, I believe. Clem is on for the rest of the day."

"Do you have concerns about confronting him? Does he have any violent tendencies?" Delaney asked. Mathias and Zoe both shook their heads.

Mathias let out a chuckle, which surprised everybody in the room. "I'd be hesitant to confront Ernest with an extra carton of ice cream. He's not exactly the friendliest of the bunch. But he's never been violent around me."

"Something about this is still off," Casper said.

Zoe glared at him. "It's the only lead we've got."

"It just feels too convenient. Too easy."

"I've never heard a detective complain about a case being too easy," Zoe said with an eye on Delaney.

"Maybe we can find something else. Something to add to the pile," Delaney said. She sorted through the stacks of paper and avoided eye contact with both her cousin and Casper.

Casper flipped through the papers again. Once he found the email log, he stopped and read through all the correspondence. "What about the email address?"

"Which one?" Mathias asked.

"McQueeney handed over his emails, exchanged with his source. It came from an email address that seems like a dummy account of sorts," Delaney said.

"What is it again?"

"Hawkeye84@gmail.com," Casper read from the page. "Could just be generic or random."

"Mathias, you know Ernest best out of all of us. Does that mean anything to you?" Zoe asked.

He shook his head. "No, but let me think." He darted out of the room and the slam of his office door shook the walls of the conference room.

"Not a quiet thinker," Casper said.

"Why not just go and talk with Ernest? Keep our hand close for now and just pick his brain about the crime instead. Maybe lean on his old crime-solving days as an excuse for the inquiry?" Delaney asked.

"It's risky. The man is volcanic if you catch him on the wrong day or even at the wrong moment. He's a lonely, bitter, old man who has as little interest in human contact as a cockroach," Zoe said.

Mathias' door slammed, and he jogged past the door and into the main lobby. The others followed his trail and stood with him in the empty entranceway. Mathias was leaning over Joanne's desk while she held up one finger in the air at him.

"One second... Okay. Sent. What's up, y'all? To what do I owe this pleasure?"

"Word association game. Ready?"

"Never pegged you as one for games, Mathias, but sure, I'm great at games. When I was a kid, we always played Clue, and it was always a surprise who—"

"Two words. Tell me if there is a connection. Ernest and Hawkeye."

Joanne almost fell out of her chair from laughing so hard. "Are you serious? That's the puzzle? Bless your hearts."

Mathias' face looked grim. "Explain."

"Oh, come on. Entertain me a little. I rarely have the upper hand in this office. You all—"

"Explain," Mathias repeated.

"Zoe, you don't know the connection either? I can't fault your friends here since they probably haven't been privy to one of Ernest's famous rants. But I expected more out of you."

"What's the connection, Joanne?" Zoe pleaded.

"Y'all need to listen when he talks sometimes. I get it. He can drone on for hours. I've got an uncle who is much of the same. But Ernest, yeah, he's got some wild opinions. Now, a lot of them involve things far before my time or things that I have no interest in. He's old as a stump in the woods, but I still follow some of it."

"Get to the point, Joanne," Mathias snarled.

"His favorite topic is re-hashing the issues with the medical issues that they tried to face on M.A.S.H.— You know, the old black and white show? Army medics and all?"

"Get to the—"

"Anybody recall the main character in the show's name? The hero that was always pulling pranks, making wisecracks, and drinking his ass off?" Joanne continued.

"Let me guess." Casper stepped in. "Hawkeye?"

CHAPTER THIRTY-ONE

CASPER WATCHED as Joanne took in the surprised faces of the park staff. Her face lit up like a Christmas tree. "Wish I had a prize for you, dear!"

Mathias glared at Joanne, then looked to Zoe. "That firms up your evidence a bit."

"Evidence?" Joanne asked. She clutched at her chest like she wore pearls. "What has Ernest gone and done this time?"

Casper stepped off to the side and nudged Delaney to follow. Once far enough away from the others, he whispered. "Tell me if I'm overthinking this but, this all could be a red herring."

"How so?" Delaney asked.

"Each domino that has fallen has led us right to Ernest. What if he's just a patsy? Somebody framed to look guilty."

"He's got two strikes against him, Casper," Delaney whispered. "The shift schedule and the email both point towards him. Nothing points anywhere else."

"Fine, I'll hold off until something else comes along. Let's see if Ernest has an explanation, anyway."

When they rejoined the group, Zoe had her hands on her hips. "A red herring?" she asked. "This room echoes like a cave. You didn't need to protect me. I can handle it."

Casper turned red. "I was just-"

Zoe shook her head. "Likely story. A little faith would go a long way here, Casper Kelly. Especially when you're trying to win my approval."

He sighed. "I'm a skeptic. That's my lean. Until the pieces all fit together, I question everything. Delaney and I had our share of disagreements during our last case. There's a benefit to having multiple minds on a case."

Zoe glared in his direction. "I'm just not sure that we're dealing with that sophisticated of a criminal, Casper," she said.

Joanne gasped. "Criminal? Y'all did not say a lick about this being related to a criminal. My oh my."

They all ignored her. "Either way, it feels like enough to ask Ernest some questions," Zoe said. She turned to Mathias. "That okay with you, sir?"

He nodded. "I support it. But I'm coming with you just in case. If I hired a criminal, I'd like to be the one to put the cuffs on him."

The oak door shook in its frame as Zoe rapped her knuckles against it. The entire house shook like a strong wind could blow it over. Casper listened for movement on the other side. Nothing but a ticking clock. Mathias tried the knob himself and then signaled toward the side of the house.

"Let's try the back door," He whispered. "His personal car is in the drive. He should be here."

The back deck of the house had seen better days. The maroon paint that once covered the boards had worn and chipped away. There was more wood than paint now. A grimy glass table with three chairs around it sat in the middle of the deck. An old umbrella with a film of pollen sat in the center, collapsed since

World War II, by the looks of it. Zoe and Mathias peered into the rear windows while Casper and Delaney stood to the side next to a woodpile in the back of the yard.

"See anything?" Mathias asked.

"Doesn't seem he's home. He left some lights on, but the TV is off. His bedroom is on the front side, right? I've only ever been in this house on a few occasions."

"Front right corner. I'll go look." Mathias pointed towards the backyard. "Look for a hide-a-key. We may need to step in. If not, I can get the spare from the office, but let's save that as a last resort."

He rounded the corner and Casper watched as his feet sunk into the wet soil that bordered the foundation of the home. He followed the instructions and scanned the backyard for anything out of the ordinary. The first few stones he turned over were actual rocks. One turned out to just be a dirt clod. Delaney walked towards the property line as it shifted from grass into the leafy forest floor. A woodpile sat to the side of the yard. Something blue caught Casper's eye.

He moved a log and placed it on the ground. Delaney joined him and looked at the hiding spot. She let out a sigh.

"What?" Casper asked.

"Strike three," she said. "Zoe, come look at this."

Casper removed the folder from the woodpile and handed it to Zoe when she arrived. She scanned through it, her eyes growing wide at each turned page. "What the…"

Mathias jogged around the bend and joined the group as well. He looked up at the others. "Did you find something?"

Zoe looked up; tears had welled up in her eyes. She nodded. "We're going to need to find Ernest. And call Detective Russo too."

"What's that there?" Mathias asked.

"It's a folder."

He raised his eyebrows. "And?"

Zoe extended it his way. "Casper found it on the log pile."

"What's inside?"

"Background information on a man. And a photo of him," Casper said.

"McQueeney?"

Zoe shook her head. "Wade Buchanon."

CHAPTER THIRTY-TWO

ANDY BLEW his whistle and watched the JV team mix with the Varsity team like younger brothers meeting their older siblings at the park. The height and skill advantage was apparent for any onlooker. There was no way to coach around that. He waved to the head coach, two pinches deep in his snuff and lost to the world. Andy jogged down towards his car. The old tin can started up on the second try after giving Andy a heart attack by sputtering out on the first.

He blazed out of the parking lot with the spirit of a man in a drag race. Within ten minutes, he was back at Cedar Pointe Condominiums. He oriented himself as he walked each hallway of the 700 building. The first floor had all units in the single digits. 707. 709. 701. Andy sprinted up the side staircase, turned right and followed the numbers on the doors, but met a dead end. He turned back past the staircase and found 712 stuck in the corner next to 717. *Some numbering system.*

Andy knocked on the door and put his ear against it. Nothing. Not even a slight movement. He slammed his palm against the door and yelled Kyle's name. Still nothing. A neighbor's blinds flittered open and somebody glared out at him. He faked a smiled at the onlooker and went back to the parking lot. Kyle's car hadn't moved. The parked car was a much more ominous sign than at first glance. *Shit. What if he's dead in there?*

Andy followed the sidewalk around the rear of the building and saw that each unit had a balcony and back deck. With his finger, he counted up and over units to deduce which was Kyle's. The sun began its descent over the horizon. Runners and walkers milled about on the paved trail below that wrapped around the algae-infested lake. He took two extra trips around the front of the building to double-check. Once he was sure that 712 was the second balcony up toward the end, Andy climbed.

The first-floor balcony was slippery from plants that were still dripping wet. Andy stood on the top railing and reached for the baseboard of the deck overhead. His legs ached from the late-night run, but he ignored the pain. The thin boards weakened his grip, but he could pull himself up, all the while cursing himself for his lack of recent upper body workouts. He swung his left foot up like a rock climber and wedged it between the bottom of the railing and the boards on the deck. He glanced back down at the ground.

Right next to the sidewalk, the less-than-helpful elderly couple from earlier, John and Margaret, were out on a walk. They stared in shock as they watched Andy's cliff-hanging climb up onto the balcony. Andy flashed a smile at them and looked out toward the lake. "He lives lakeside. Thanks for your help!" He shouted.

The Scottish Terrier barked back in its familiar growling melody. He didn't turn to see their reactions. Two minutes later, he brushed himself off on what he hoped was Kyle's back deck. A circular glass patio table sat with two green flimsy plastic chairs facing the lake. Two plants, or the remains of oft-forgotten plants, hung from the overhead rafters. A flipped over mountain bike sat parked atop its handlebars next to a small exterior closet with chipped paint. He looked back down out on the lake. *Nice view. Not half bad.*

A large glass window and screen door led into the main living area. Andy cupped his eyes and looked into the room. Old newspapers and books covered a tan sofa. A video game controller sat in the center of the coffee table that stood in front of a flat-screen TV. In the distance, Andy could see a kitchen table with stacks of books and Kyle's backpack on top of it. One chair laid sideways on the ground, but nothing else was out of place. Andy reached for the handle of the screen door.

It slid open and Andy stepped inside. Security clearly wasn't the chief concern of residents on the second floor. After all, what kind of maniac is going to climb in through the back porch. He surveyed the room for a carton of cigarettes that could help calm his nerves, but nothing was in sight. *Me. I'm the maniac.*

The rank smell of a room in desperate need of a vacuum and wipe down overwhelmed his senses. The scent reminded Andy of his frat house in college. Stale beer and microwaved food. Ramen noodle wrappers sat on the counter. The sink was full of grimy dishes, piled up like a homemade game of Tetris. *Better than a dead body, right?* He crept toward the hallway. *What if I'm disturbing a crime scene? What if I frame myself? Isn't that how all this works? Down, down I go.*

Andy stepped into the hallway and saw there were three doors. All shut. He put his ear to each of them. Nothing. Not a sound. With a sigh, he started with the door at the end of the hallway. He turned the knob and edged it open. No light snuck out from inside. As he swung it all the way open, it relieved him to find a tiny, messy bathroom with a towel that looked damp. He put his fingers on the toothbrush. Damp. Somebody's been here.

Back in the hallway, Andy opened the door to his right with great caution. He tiptoed his way into the doorframe. A queen-sized bed sat in the middle of the room, made with military precision. Two pillows that had no impressions on them sat atop the mattress. No signs of life. Like something out of a still-life painting of a hotel room. Just missing the mints on the pillow.

The walls stood bare aside from a wooden clock. The ticking sound of the second hand echoed through the cavernous, empty room. The metronomic sound mirrored Andy's breath. In and out. In and out. Two windows looked out into the courtyard. As he looked out of them, he saw the old couple with the devilish dog returning from their walk. He considered waving or giving them the finger, but decided against it. He opened the closet but found nothing. No old clothes or storage space filled with leftover crap. But that made sense. Kyle was single. He didn't have to account for the every-other-weekend swell that two visiting kids provided with all of their crap to take up Andy's space. The room was barren. Too empty. *Maybe he ran for it. Left his car and booked it out of here. Hopped on a train to Mexico. Can't blame him. Wait, do trains go to Mexico from Raleigh?*

Andy left the closet doors open like when his kids used to be afraid of monsters before bedtime. *Here, see? There's nothing in there. I'll leave it open just in case.* As he crept back toward the hallway, something crashed in the living room. He cupped his ear but heard nothing else. He stepped out into the hallway. Turned toward the kitchen. Something heavy crashed into his knees. He fell like a sack of bricks to the floor. His head thumped against the plush, stained carpet. Pain raced through his legs. With his face in the rug, he turned to size up his attacker. They wore a mask that sent shivers down Andy's spine. *What the hell?*

CHAPTER THIRTY-THREE

THE HEATED DISCUSSION on what to do next camouflaged the crunch of gravel under boots. Casper, Delaney, Zoe, and Mathias stood in a circle, hands-on-hips, and argued about the path forward. The clearing of a throat interrupted them. They all turned to see Ernest Henley standing in his driveway grinning at them.

"Did I miss the invite to a party or something? I don't turn seventy until next fall, y'all." His eyes turned toward the folder in Mathias' hands. "What's that you got there?"

"You didn't hide it well, Ernest," Zoe said.

"I didn't hide anything. What is it? Hand it here."

Mathias held it tight. "It's a folder with incriminating evidence that inclines me to put cuffs on you right now unless you start talking."

Ernest scoffed. "I've never seen that before in my life. Where'd you find it?"

"In your woodpile."

"In my woodpile? That's the world's worst hiding spot, Zoe. That makes no sense."

Casper watched the man's expression. It was sincere shock. And he had a point. Why would somebody hide something like that in plain sight? Why would he have kept it at all?

"Are you saying you have no idea what this is?" Mathias asked.

"Swear on my life." He tossed his keys onto the table. "What exactly do you think I did here, Mathias? I'd appreciate it if you just came out and said it instead of pussyfooting around like a—"

"I'm inclined to believe that you are responsible for the recent rash of Bigfoot sightings and the assault on Wade Buchanon."

Ernest crossed his arms and grinned at them. "Those are some big accusations. Care to explain how you came to this conclusion?"

"There are a few peculiarities, to say the least."

"You all have been looking into me?"

"We gathered some evidence from the man captured last night in the Bigfoot costume. After looking it over, we decided we had questions to ask you. So, we came here. Then we found this." Zoe tapped the folder. "Now, it looks an awful lot like you have an early retirement on the horizon. I hear they play old *M.A.S.H.* reruns in prison at least, Hawkeye."

Ernest pulled at his beard and looked down. "Look, it's not... I know nothing about that folder. Nor do I have anything to do with the beating of that man on Saturday."

"I'd like to point out you didn't deny your involvement in the Bigfoot hoax." Casper said.

Ernest shook his head. His face lost color. "It's not what you think. Look, you've got to believe me. Let's sit down and talk about this. Please." He motioned toward the chairs on his back deck and then sat. Mathias and the others followed. Casper stood off to the side to have an optimal angle of Ernest's face throughout the makeshift interrogation.

Mathias pulled the photo of Wade Buchanon out of the folder and placed it in front of Ernest. "Explain."

Ernest pushed it away. "I've got no guilt over what happened to that man. But the other stuff, well, I can explain."

Zoe glanced at Mathias, then spoke just above a whisper. "Raleigh PD traced the IP addresses of the emails that were received by our recently imprisoned Bigfoot impersonator. All signs point towards your house here, Ernest. Care to explain that?"

Casper admired her bluff. If he didn't know better, he would've believed it without hesitation. He noticed Delaney hide a smile by putting her hand over her mouth. Ernest let out a sigh that could blow down a mountain and then slumped over in his chair. "Ah, shit. That technology bullshit. You can trace anything anywhere these days. That's why I didn't want to use it in the first place." He scraped at his scalp. "But the money-"

"Elaborate," Mathias said.

Ernest exhaled and leaned back in his chair so far the front legs kicked up. "I got a letter in the mail. It offered me a truckload of cash to share some information. Digitally."

"Digitally?" Zoe asked.

"Like on the web. I made an email and got everything set up. Had to have my cousin walk me through the steps and all. To be honest, I never thought the money would show."

"But it did?" Casper asked.

"Without fail. Hidden in the same spot you just found that folder. Inside the woodpile."

"Just plain cash? Nothing else?" Zoe asked.

"White envelope sealed with a sticker. No words."

"And what did you have to do for these envelopes full of cash, Ernest?" Mathias spoke in a growl.

"I told you! I shared information. Sent our shift schedules each month, among other things. After the first few sightings got reported, I learned that if I circled certain days, I could make sure nothing happened on my watch. So, I did that. Sometimes I let them know when there were events in the park or stuff like that. Like when the group camps were full of Boy Scouts or if we had volunteers starting early in the morning."

"And the cameras?" Casper asked.

Ernest glared up at him and sighed. "Yeah, I sent that over too. I knew that would be key information. I thought it would be easy enough for them to steer clear but-"

"So, you didn't tell them to trigger the camera?"

"Son, do I look dumb to you?"

"Why did you agree to this, Ernest?"

"The first reason was money. The first ask was just a copy of our schedule here. I thought, no harm, no foul. And the money was more than I deserved. But after that, I tried to call it off."

"How so?"

"I told them I was out. Done."

"And?"

"And they responded with an envelope full of photographs of my grandkids. At school. Playing on the jungle gym. Walking in the park. It spooked me. The instructions said that if I played along, I would be a rich man and nobody would get hurt. I didn't ask questions beyond that."

"And what about Wade Buchanon? How did he fit into this?" Zoe pushed.

Ernest sighed. "Hand on my heart, I had nothing to do with that man's injuries."

"Where were you Saturday morning?"

"Asleep in my bed. Alone. Unless you can convince old Trotter to speak English instead of meow, I don't have any way to verify it. Except that it's the god-damned truth."

"Then how can you explain this folder full of evidence?"

"I can't."

"Do you know who is calling the shots? Who was sending you that money?" Casper asked.

"If I knew, I'd be the first one to report it to the authorities. I guessed it was somebody from a case I worked in the past. Somebody I put away in prison for a while that was back to come and wreck my life."

Mathias reached for his phone. "We'll need to have Detective Russo question you."

Ernest pursed his lips. "If you say so. Look, I'll walk away from everything if you can guarantee their safety."

"I'm sure we can work something out if this all checks out as you say it will. I'll call her."

Mathias stepped away. Casper thought about the placement. The use of the same location as the money drops. Like a threat. Or a connection. Something tying this all into one neat little bow. Casper joined them at the table and looked at Ernest. "What kind of sticker?"

"Huh?" Ernest said.

"You said they sealed the envelope of money with a sticker."

He nodded.

"What kind of sticker?"

"It was a little fox."

CHAPTER THIRTY-FOUR

"KYLE? WHAT THE HELL?" Andy cried out.

Kyle removed the tattered *Scream* Halloween mask and smiled at Andy. "I'm sorry, man, I thought you were somebody else."

"And you attacked me just in case? Did you think I was wearing a Fox costume?"

"After what happened to that guy on the trail, I wasn't taking any chances." Kyle extended a hand to help him up. "How's your leg?"

Andy sat up with his back against the flimsy wall of the hall-way. "I'll live. A limp will be a perfect conversation starter with the ladies." He glared at Kyle. "I tried calling you, man. What the hell?"

Kyle stepped into the kitchen and dug through his freezer. "I ditched my phone. Figured that was the only way The Fox knew to find me, so I tossed it in the Eno River." He handed Andy a bag of frozen peas. "Sorry, I don't have an ice pack. This may help the swelling."

"You're losing it, man," Andy said. He braced himself and tried to stand up. His knees wobbled, but they soon remembered how to work and he thrust himself into one of the kitchen chairs.

"No, I think you haven't woken up yet." Kyle shook his head and paced around the kitchen. "The Fox is no joke. They mean business. And they may still think it was you!" Andy noticed that Kyle's eyes were bloodshot but decided not to mention it.

"No, I think that's settled." Andy cleared his throat. "I, uh, I did a job yesterday."

Kyle's eyes grew wide. He paced around the room. The nervousness was palpable. "You what? Why?" Kyle huffed in anger. "Andy, you're an idiot! I told you to lie low—"

"I wanted to see if things were normal," Andy explained.

"And? How normal is it if you had to come break into my goddamned house?"

"It was the same. I mean, almost. The job is done, and the money went into my account like always. The job was just slightly different."

"How different?" Kyle stopped and stared.

"Different part of the park. Different instructions."

"Different instructions? The Fox doesn't do different instructions. Are you sure it was the same person?"

"Same number. Yeah…" Andy glanced at the redness on his leg. "I had to pull something out of the bag and hide it in plain sight."

"And you looked at it?"

"It wasn't like a weapon or anything like that."

Kyle rubbed his chin. "What was it?"

"Are you sure you want to know? I don't want to hear your paranoid ramblings about how this is implicating you further."

"Just tell me." Kyle sat, but his leg jack-hammered on the carpet. "Drugs? A gun?"

"No, man!" Andy laughed. "Do you think I would be this calm if I just had my hands on a brick of heroin or a Glock? Hell no. It was just a folder. Bunch of photographs and documents inside."

"A folder? What the hell?"

"Dude, I know better than to ask questions after what you told me. I also know better than to stick around after I make a drop and watch the god-damned pickup." He shook his head. "My god that was a dumb move, Kyle."

Kyle's face stiffened. "I never said it was a smart idea. But at least I know what I'm up against. I had this nagging feeling that I was constantly being set up. Like this was a sting, and we were just racking up the charges against us with each gig."

"Speaking of that. I thought long and hard about everything that is at stake. I think you should go to the police."

Kyle laughed. "Are you crazy? Why in the hell would I do that?"

"You're clearly falling apart at the seams here, dude. Not showing up for work. Lurking around your apartment in a fucking Halloween costume!" Andy shouted.

"And you'd like me to waltz into the police station and say what?" He pressed his hands against the kitchen counter and stared daggers at Andy. "I was a drug smuggler and I think my drug lord is a bad person."

"I wouldn't lead with that but..."

"Then what? What is the benefit of walking into certain doom?"

"You said you saw their face."

"Who?"

"The Fox."

"So?"

"You could provide a sketch. I don't know how it all works, but it feels like enough to trade for some sort of deal. What's that called, Mr. English Teacher?"

"Clemency?"

"Yeah, bingo. You go in there and ask for clemency. Beg for their mercy and offer to give up a criminal's identity in exchange for your freedom. It's the safest way out."

"But—"

"And we don't even know if we are smuggling drugs or guns or what. There's got to be something in the law that helps us out there. Unknowing participants or something like that." Andy shrugged. "We are just transporters. As guilty as an Uber driver that picks somebody up from a murder scene. Taking things from one place to another. Doing a job. I have never looked inside a backpack until last night. Have you?"

"No, but—"

"See, you only know what you know." Andy lifted the bag of peas and plopped it onto the counter. "They hired you to drop things off from time to time. To use your running as camouflage and blend into the scenery of Umstead Park. How is that a crime?"

"It was far away, I'm not sure that I can provide enough—"

"Anything is a start." Andy forced a smile. "Plus, I don't see why you'd even mention that you were doing anything besides going for a run. It's a believable story. You were running in the park like you often do, and you came around a bend in the trail and *bam*. You hid out and watched things go down and then got the hell out of there."

Kyle calmed down. "And how do I explain leaving without helping the guy?"

"I don't know, dude. Say you were about to call 911 when you heard an ambulance or something. Say you were in shock. You're the wordsmith. Think of something."

"Okay, I see your point but let me take you down a rabbit hole that I've been spiraling towards lately. What if The Fox is a cop?" Kyle paused and waited for Andy to react. Nothing came. "Cops know a lot about how to evade suspicion. In crime shows, the cops are just as guilty as the crooks. What if I walk into the station and the uniformed officer that takes my statement is the same sonofabitch that I saw beat the crap out of that old dude?"

"You've seen way too much TV. That's a borderline impossibility." Andy laughed.

Kyle was stoic. "It's not impossible. I'm just trying to watch my ass here, you know?"

"Look, I know you're worried. I have been too. Ever since you came to practice ranting about this brutal crime you witnessed, I keep thinking about my kids. Watching my back. Thinking that I need to get them to safety. Thinking that my dumb ass put them in harm's way! I can't live like this, man."

Kyle stared at the floor.

"Please? At least consider it."

The whir of the ceiling fan was the only sound left in the room. Andy stared at his friend. His colleague. His partner-in-crime. He put on his most pitiful look. He let his fear show for the first time. Kyle let out a deep sigh. "Need to get you off the soccer field and coaching our debate team, damn. All right. I'll do it on one condition," Kyle said.

"What's that?"

"I also get to tell them about the crazy idiot that scaled the back of my condo to break into my house."

Andy put both his wrists together and held them out towards Kyle. "If I get to choose which prison they send me to, I'd like to go somewhere warm."

CHAPTER THIRTY-FIVE

THE TEMPERATURE FELL as the sun set, a swift reminder that summer had passed and winter crept closer with its bleak, dark mornings and barren deciduous trees. Zoe considered that the chill that crept up her spine may not be from the weather, but from the bitter chaos of the evening's events. After Casper and Delaney left to check on Hoagie, she watched Detective Russo finish her interview with Ernest Henley. As much as she wanted to be a fly on that wall, it made sense that Russo insisted no park staff be present. Bias can creep in far too easily. Zoe leaned with her lower back against her truck, an attempt at calm that wouldn't fool a preschooler.

Russo smiled when she stepped out of the residence and saw Zoe waiting for her. "I would've put money on you waiting for us to wrap up. You're a persistent one, you know?"

"I'm sorry, I—"

Russo held up a hand. "It's a compliment, Zoe. Do you know how many LEOs would write this off and get bundled up next to a fire or be halfway through a six-pack by now?" Russo smiled. "You care. Never apologize for that. It's not lost on me and it's sure as hell not lost on your supervisor."

"Mathias?"

"I know you think everybody has you pegged as the bottom of the food chain around here but... well... hang in there," she grinned. "But you didn't come here for a pep talk. You want to know what I learned from old Ernest Henley."

Zoe nodded. "Did he do it?"

Russo nodded towards Zoe's truck. "Mind if we step inside and crank the heat? I'm a southerner at heart and this fall weather is frigid for me."

Zoe unlocked the truck and hopped in. Russo followed, the top of her glassy black hair grazing the ceiling of the tiny cab.

"It'll take a minute to turn over to heat," Zoe said with a bashful smile.

Russo nodded. "Police cruisers are just as old. I'm used to it. Anyway, you asked if he did it. The answer is yes and no."

"How so?"

"We built off your initial interview of Ernest and expanded our search a bit. I had a tech-savvy member of our forensics team remote access his laptop, and thanks to his senior-citizen aversion to technology, it provided us with a slew of unprotected clues. Apparently, he thought his password at the login screen was enough to prevent anybody from finding anything incriminating. He was sorely mistaken."

"What did you find?"

"Well, first off, Ernest did not lie to you, as far as we can tell. He was a patsy. A middle-man in it for some extra cash. He shared with us the photos of his grandchildren that he said came in the envelope, but without the original instructions, it's meaningless. Anybody could have printed them off his Facebook page at a local CVS. We have them bagged and will dust for fingerprints, but I wouldn't hold your breath."

Zoe ran her hands through her ratty blonde hair. "Geez."

"He leaked information. Privileged information that would only be valuable to a small subset of people, but nonetheless. It will be up to Mathias and the rest of the higher-ups in the State Park system to look into all that and decide an appropriate punishment. My guess is that Ernest is looking at a forced retirement, but again, that's not my wheelhouse. Anyway, the larger concern is whoever is tugging Ernest's puppet strings, so to speak."

"Agreed. I'll admit that I still don't see how it all connects."

Russo let out a sigh. "You're not alone on that ledge, lady. We're still working on pulling at the right threads. Unfortunately, I have a lot of cases on my plate and my captain is pushing resources towards other matters since it looks like Wade Buchanon is going to pull through. Despite his recovery, he has no memory of the incident, so it's not like he's going to pop up with an ID in the next few hours. If he does, all the better. But again, nobody is holding their breath. Anyway, I know this hurts to hear, but my superiors will soon put this case on the back burner."

Zoe looked at her muddy boots on the dirt-stained floor mat. "Never thought of Raleigh as a dangerous place with all these cases..."

Russo chuckled. "Not exactly dangerous, but minor crimes are happening everywhere and we don't have a big staff. A lot like y'all here at the park, right? You can only cover so many miles of trail between your staff. Gotta prioritize however upper management decides."

Zoe's mind was still three steps behind, stuck on something. "Do you have any inklings about the puppeteer as you described them?"

"We know a few things. First, they are smart. They used dummy IP addresses and email accounts to set up everything. No paper trail besides the cash that Ernest was getting. We found an envelope similar to what Ernest had when we searched McQueeney's mess of an apartment. Not just smart with tech, but smart in being organized. They planned everything with precision. That's not everybody's bag of chips, so to speak."

Russo and Zoe watched as Ernest peaked through the blinds in his bedroom window. The man couldn't sneak up on a deaf sloth if he wanted to, but Zoe understood the unease caused by an extended police presence in your driveway.

Russo continued. "Second, this is bigger than it seems on the surface. I had the bagged evidence from McQueeney's on my desk when one of my colleagues from our Narcotics division came by. He'd heard about what we found. He showed me a small bag of heroin that was sealed with... want to guess?"

"A fox sticker?"

"You're smart as a whip. You've got it," Russo gave her a light pat on the shoulder.

"So, what does it mean?"

"Well, as I said, we're piecing it together now. There's a lot of puzzle pieces that do not seem to align with one another. On one hand, we've got an idiot parading around in a Bigfoot costume. On the other, we have a recent uptick in drug cases and arrests. Add in a corrupt Park Ranger and this is one odd jumble of facts. The only thread connecting all the dots is the sticker."

Zoe stared out through the windshield. The dirt and grime from her commute to the office had built up a layer of filth around the wiper's range. She let her eyes shift focus onto Ernest's house. The old tannish-brown cabin needed a fresh coat of paint. Some TLC would go a long way in fixing up the side yard too. Logs sat in a clumsy pile along the back line of the property, the lower half of the pyramid brown and worn with age, while the recent additions were too fresh to burn.

"Zoe?" Russo interrupted.

"Yeah, sorry. I was just—"

"No bother, it's a lot to take in. Especially when it's all happening in this little slice of paradise that you call home."

"I doubt anybody has ever described Umstead as paradise, but—"

"Do me a favor? Sleep on this. Go home, let your mind rest and get some shut-eye. It does wonders for the brain, and this mess won't clear up without you in the meantime. Maybe something will fall into place while you're in the shower. Amazing how that happens, right?"

Zoe nodded. "Thank you, Chandler. I appreciate your candor and care with all of this. It's admirable."

"Aw, dear. You're talking to the mirror there. I am only sending out what I'm getting back. You're a hell of a law enforcement officer, Zoe Watts. You ever get sick of the trees and want to find your way into an over-air-conditioned office with a bunch of men with masculinity complexes, you let me know."

Zoe smiled and watched Russo leave. She let out a deep exhale and reversed out of the drive. She took the long way home, all the while trying to force the puzzle pieces to fit into the frame. It was a fool's errand without knowing what the end result was supposed to be. Without progress, she let her mind wander and follow along with the CD that played on repeat for months. For a minute, she let her mind drift into the lyrics. After all, she could relate. *Looks like we're in for nasty weather...*

The bad moon had risen.

CHAPTER THIRTY-SIX

THE DOOR SLAMMED SHUT behind Zoe, but not before she let in a stiff breeze from the world outside. Delaney shivered and reached for her sweatshirt. Casper stayed slumped onto the couch, still reeling from the events of the day. Hoagie raced to greet his new best friend.

Casper's mind moved a mile a minute. His thoughts spiraled, dancing from the worst-case scenarios to possible harmless explanations. Nothing stuck. Something was off.

"How did things go with Russo?" Delaney asked.

"Hello to you too, Laney. Yeesh," Zoe said with a grin. "Just a vehicle for information these days, aren't I?"

Delaney rushed up with a hug. "You're not a vehicle for anything. Except for maybe smelly armpits."

"Grow up, Laney. I eventually found deodorant that works. Want to sniff?" Zoe asked.

Gil entered the room and smiled. "No comment on the armpits. But I echo the question. Lay it on us."

As Zoe shared her summary of the events and Russo's interview with Ernest, Casper started scribbling on a notepad. He poked at it with his pen and then wrote. Delaney peered over his shoulder, but she gave up trying to decode his horrendous handwriting. Zoe finished, let out a sigh, and threw herself into the tan armchair in the corner of the room. She looked like a deflated balloon.

"Maybe Russo is right. Sleep could do us all some good. It's been a marathon of a day," Delaney said.

"Can I ask a question?" Gil interrupted.

"Yes, but only one, Gil," Zoe said with a smile.

"Well, more of a statement, for now. I am, as you never would have surmised, stuck on the Bigfoot angle. I cannot see how that, er, prank, is a logical move."

"How so?"

"Well, it is rather absurd. Is it not? Why Bigfoot?"

"It's a misdirect," Casper said. "A distraction from the actual events. From how it sounds, it's a distraction to avoid detection of something related to drugs."

"Yes, I recall your earlier statement of that notion, Casper. What I am asking is, specifically, why did they choose Bigfoot? Why not set fires in the woods or vandalize the bathrooms with spray paint? There are simpler options that would draw the ire and attention of the staff."

"It's a valid question, Gil," Zoe said with a sigh. "We have more questions than answers at the moment. But it still irks me."

"What does?" Delaney asked.

"The location."

"Like, where we found McQueeney in the costume?" Delaney said.

Zoe shook her head. "No, just the fact that any of this took place within Umstead. It doesn't add up."

"There's a phrase from an old science fiction book that has always stuck with me that applies here," Casper said. *"Maps were the first form of misdirection, for what is a map but a way of emphasizing some things and making others invisible?* Have you ever looked at a map of Umstead online?"

Zoe shrugged. "Sure, it's just a landmass with a few marked trails through it."

"Exactly, it's a cloak." Casper smiled. "It's the perfect environment for avoiding detection, so long as the folks policing the area have their hands full with something else."

"But there are countless parks in North Carolina. Some are bigger. Hell, there are ones with less staff! Entire forests that are uninhabited and unexplored," Zoe said.

"Are any of them within earshot of two major cities? Umstead is smack dab in the middle. The perfect location to use as a playground." Casper met Zoe's eyes as he continued. "One hundred years ago, prohibition brought about a slew of new criminals who used clever tactics to avoid suspicion. One of the most popular? Brewing in the woods. When they were somewhere only passable by foot, it added a layer of security."

"Yeah but—"

"And one of the most famous bootlegger stories, one that even made its way up north to my high school, was cow shoes."

"Cow shoes?" Gil asked.

Casper grinned. "Bootleggers made these attachments to the bottoms of their shoes that made their footprints in the soil look like the hoofprint of a cow. As the law tried to track the operations through the forests, they had to discern which hoof prints were real and which were a trick. It's a lot like this scheme here."

"So, you're saying the Bigfoot sightings, in this case, are cow shoes? That's a sentence that makes my head spin, Casper," Zoe said.

He laughed. "It's confusing, but to put it simply, we're still chasing down the wrong tracks. Whoever this mastermind is, they want us to follow the Bigfoot charade until we come up empty. If we look in that direction, we'll miss them cleaning up whatever bigger activity was going on here."

Zoe stood and paced around the room. "But we've got little to go off of. We have stickers that match across the board. Little foxes. Clever, I'll admit that much. But this fox wants their tracks covered."

"And if you follow the tracks, there's a solid chance this fox leads us to answers as to whatever happened to Wade Buchanon. The dots connect, Zoe," Casper said.

Zoe sighed. "So, how in the world do we catch him?"

"Simply put, we set him a trap. If he takes the bait or gets caught on his own, we'll be that much closer to an answer."

Gil nodded. "Just remember, a fox is a clever animal. You'll have to outwit it to make this work."

"If we were hunting an actual fox, you'd be right. But we're looking for a human. A terrible, violent human. When it all boils down, it's a hell of a lot easier to catch a human than a fox."

CHAPTER THIRTY-SEVEN

DEW CLUNG to blades of grass along the sidewalk that led toward the station. Kyle moved like a man approaching the gallows. His feet were heavy. Like blocks of cement instead of shoes. His stomach grew sour and he could feel bile in his throat. He let out a deep breath and pulled the door of the station open.

The noise overwhelmed him at first. Phones ringing and people milling about from one place to another. A uniformed officer who looked to be the same age as one of Kyle's honors students sat behind the front desk and greeted the visitor with a big, goofy smile.

"Can I help you, sir?"

The *sir* sent shivers down Kyle's twenty-six-year-old spine. His mouth had never been so dry. Like he'd just taken in a mouthful of sand. "Yes, uh, Officer Agnew," He read from his badge. "I need to speak to somebody about something I saw."

"Sure thing! And what is this regarding? I just need to know which officer to contact." The baby-faced man looked like a child playing dress-up.

"Uh, I saw a man. In Umstead State Park. He got hurt."

"Oh no, like a sprained ankle? Yikes!" Officer Agnew made an exaggerated face.

"No, uh, like he got beat up." Kyle said while doing his best to shove off the images of the bloody scene he'd witnessed.

"Let me check into that, one second. You said it was at Umstead?"

Kyle nodded. Officer Harrison picked up his phone and mumbled into it for a few minutes. Kyle leaned up against the counter and his legs grew weaker. He opted for the worn vinyl chair that had one leg shorter than the rest.

"Sir?" Officer Harrison asked.

That sir again. Kyle stood and met the officer who had come from around the desk.

"You can follow me; I'll show you back to Detective Russo. She's waiting for you."

The two-minute walk felt like a marathon. Every person they passed stared daggers at Kyle. Sweat beaded on his neck and dripped down his t-shirt. He glanced at the corkboard they passed, half-expecting to see his and Andy's face on printouts next to the rest of *America's Most Wanted* but there was nothing besides a small list of upcoming overtime opportunities and the NC State Football schedule.

The march ended. He ushered Kyle into an empty interrogation room five degrees cooler than the rest of the station. Goosebumps prickled his skin. He nodded at his escort and waited alone. The silence gnawed at him with each passing second.

Fifteen minutes later, an attractive older woman with dark hair stepped into the room. She stood at least six feet tall. Maybe taller. She smiled and signaled for him to take a seat. "Hi, I'm Detective Russo. I appreciate you coming in." Her smile had faded. "Officer Harrison said that you have some information regarding a case that I'm working."

"Uh, yes. I saw something."

"Great, well let's start with the basics." Russo pulled out a pen and a notepad. "What's your name?"

"Kyle Pittman."

"Nice to meet you, Kyle." She scribbled something on the page. "And where is it you work?"

"I'm an English teacher at Pine Hills High School."

Russo grinned. "The most underpaid profession in the world, am I right?"

Kyle chuckled. "You can say that again."

"So, Kyle." Each time she said his name, it reminded him of a kindergartener being held out of recess for eating crayons. "Did you see or hear something at school?"

"No, ma'am. I saw something in the park."

"And which park is this, Kyle?" Russo held her pen still on the notepad.

"Umstead State Park. I thought the officer at the door told you."

She chuckled. "He provided the basics, but I like to be thorough. Don't you, Kyle?"

"Uh, I guess."

"Wonderful. Okay, so, what were you doing in Umstead State Park?"

"I was, uh, running." Kyle nodded. "Just out for a run, you know?"

"Exercise is important. That's an early hour though, do you often run that early?"

"Sometimes. When I need to get it done before school or something. I'm an early bird."

"Not me." She shook her head. "I'm far from a morning lark. I am the night owl hooting at you while you're trying to sleep." Russo laughed to herself. "So, tell me what you saw, Kyle."

"Well, I was coming down the big hill that you hit when you leave the main parking lot and head out on the wider trails."

"The bridle trails? Which side of the park is this?"

"Off Harrison Ave? I don't know if that's Cary or Raleigh. I parked outside the gate since it was before the park opened. I know that's technically against the rules but—"

She smiled at him. "We'll make an exception on that one, Kyle."

"So, I came down the big hill and saw what I thought was this… uh… creature jump on top of some other guy."

Russo was calm. She took careful notes. "Okay, can you describe either person?"

"Well, I mean, the victim was like middle-aged. Maybe late forties? He looked like he was on a run too, but I never saw him actually running. But yeah, just a normal, average guy. Medium build. Brown hair that looked like it was receding."

"Great. And you said you saw a creature, Kyle? That sounds scary."

"Yes, well, at first I thought it was a creature, but then I got a little closer… and…" Kyle's lips couldn't find the words. His throat was raw.

Detective Russo smiled and put her hand up in the air. "How about I grab you a glass of water and then we can continue. Does that work?"

Kyle nodded, and then the detective disappeared. The room was still cold. He shivered, either from nerves or from the frosty air that pumped through the vent in the floor. He let out a deep exhale. *All the practice with Andy paid off. Except, why does she keep saying my name?* He replayed all of his answers in his mind. He had yet to implicate himself. If he played it right, he could walk out of the station scot-free. Like a normal runner in the park who had no connection to the vicious person who beat that man half to death.

The detective left the room for what felt like fifteen minutes. Kyle stirred in his chair and looked at his hands. When he was about to knock on the door to ask for the promised glass of water,

Detective Russo rejoined him inside the room. She handed him a bottle of water, which he gulped down without a word.

"Great. Okay, so where were we, Kyle? You got closer to the crime scene?"

Kyle nodded. "I could see that it wasn't a creature but a person in a weird costume."

"Okay, what kind of costume did it look like?"

"It was a fox."

"A fox?"

"But a small one."

"A baby fox?"

"No, just that like the person was small, I guess."

"Okay, that's great, Kyle. Details are important. So, you saw a small person in fox costume beat the middle-aged man who was running?"

"Yes."

"And you watched?"

Kyle's voice cracked. "I know I should have done something, but I was so scared. Shocked. It was like a bad dream. I stared at it in pure horror, but I froze. I couldn't move."

"Lots of people find that their bodies let them down. Minds too. Fight or flight, right, Kyle?"

"Uh-huh."

"And is that it? That's what you wanted to report today?" The detective looked at the two-way mirror that sat in front of Kyle.

"No, there's a little more."

"Okay. What else, Kyle?"

"The costume. It had this, like, head. A fox head. And during the fight, it fell off."

Detective Russo sat up in her chair. "Do you mean you saw the person's face who was attacking Wade Buchanon?"

"If that's the old guy, yeah."

"And what did he look like? Can you give us some details?"

"Yeah, I have a good memory. Hard to forget something like that."

"Great, Kyle. That's helpful."

"But there's one thing you're getting wrong, detective."

"And what's that, Kyle?"

"It wasn't a he. The person in the fox costume was a woman."

CHAPTER THIRTY-EIGHT

ZOE'S KNEES buckled beneath her as she listened to Kyle Pittman's statement. The words echoed through her brain like a leaf falling from a tree limb, dancing through the sky before it lands on the ground. Her eyes glazed over as she glared at the young man who had just dropped an atomic bomb on the entire case. *A woman?* Zoe's reflection looked back at her in the tiny observation room as she glared through the two-way mirror.

Detective Russo's call had urged Zoe and Mathias to head towards the station for an urgent update. A rookie officer who looked to be no older than fifteen had put them in the observation room and left them alone to watch. Mathias cautioned that nothing substantial was likely to come from the discussion. Still, Zoe hoped for answers. For progress. However, this was not the answer she'd expected.

Mathias glanced at her with a particular look that she did not envy. One woman at the park that came to mind right away. One who lived nearby. One who knew the trails and was conveniently among the first on the scene. Zoe gulped. She averted her eyes and watched as Russo put the eyewitness on the spot.

Detective Russo continued the questioning inside. "A woman?"

Kyle nodded and drank the rest of his water. His methodical movements were disturbing to Zoe, who wanted to wring the man's neck to get answers as quickly as possible.

"Can you describe her?" Russo asked with her pen on her notepad and a winning smile across her face.

"She was pale. Freckles on her skin," Kyle said. "I was far away, but yeah. Red hair. Like fire-red."

"And you said she was petite?"

"Small, petite. Yes. Thin. Runner's build, maybe? Like I said—"

Mathias whispered under his breath as the realization dawned on him. "Shit." Zoe couldn't stop staring.

Russo continued. "And you saw this petite red-headed woman assault Wade Buchanon?"

"She was in a rage. Angry is an understatement. He must have pissed her off, or maybe they knew each other before or something. I don't know."

"Okay, one last time to make sure I got it all, then I will have to step out for a moment to call this into my colleagues. You were running in Umstead, saw a red-headed woman in a fox costume attacking Wade Buchanon from a hiding spot, and then what?" Russo spoke with a silent urgency.

"What do you mean?" Kyle's brow raised.

"Did you leave? Did the woman in the fox costume leave? Help me understand how this all wraps up..."

"I ran out of the woods and back up the trail to my car. I was scared as hell. I drove out of there like my hair was on fire. I was ashamed that I didn't do anything, so I hesitated in approaching you all about it. I know it was wrong, but..." His voice trailed off.

"Well, all things aside, we're grateful that you could now. Hang tight a minute and I'll be right back."

Russo stepped into the hallway. Zoe and Mathias soon followed. The look on her face evaporated when she saw their faces.

"Sound like somebody you know?" Russo asked.

Zoe nodded. "We need to get to the park. Now."

Russo was already moving towards the parking lot. "Follow me. Hope you've got a lead foot because they don't call me Earnhardt around here for nothing." She shifted into a jog and busted through the rear doors of the station.

Mathias was already out in front of them and hopping into his truck. Zoe jumped in as he turned over the engine. It roared to life. Zoe fumbled for the radio and then paused, staring at her co-pilot. Mathias nodded. "Smart move," he said. "No radio. Call Delaney and Casper directly. Tell them we're on the way."

Russo pulled out in front of them and shouted from her open window. "No sirens. Can't spook anybody. Let's go!"

Mathias floored it and followed Russo's cruiser as it peeled out of the lot in a cloud of smoke. The smell of burnt rubber stung Zoe's nostrils as it crept through the air system of the old truck. She let out a cough as she waited for her call to go through. Delaney's phone went straight to voicemail, so Zoe tried Casper. He picked up on the first ring.

"Casper! Get Delaney and meet us at the Visitor's Center. Don't let any of the staff leave."

"What's going on? What—"

"Don't answer questions and just hang tight. Mathias and I will be there in ten minutes. With back up."

"Better make that five!" Mathias said with a grin as he pressed the gas pedal to the floorboard. The old truck roared to life, and the doors shook.

"Casper?" Zoe said.

"Yeah?"

"Don't let any of the staff leave."

Zoe hung up and watched Mathias shadow Russo's methodical movements through the traffic on Route 70. They passed the Crabtree Valley Mall and then a half-mile stretch of furniture stores and car dealerships. Cars shifted lanes to avoid the oncoming speed demons and often rubbernecked at the passing blurs to piece together what had just happened. But even Zoe struggled to comprehend the pieces that sat before her. When they all added up, there was little else to feel but betrayal.

"Did you ever suspect her?" Zoe asked.

Mathias stared out into the traffic, and after a long pause, shook his head. "No."

"Me either."

"But something like this? Whatever this is? I wouldn't suspect anybody. I thought… well, never mind all that. Let's just hope this ends quietly."

Zoe fixed her eyes on the road in front of her. Russo dodged traffic like it was a video game and she was impervious to injury. Zoe admired the confidence the detective had behind the wheel. *Wonder if Laney can drive like this. Maybe it's part of the detective's exam.*

The turnoff into the main entrance of the park appeared to their left, across oncoming traffic. Russo didn't hesitate. She gunned it past the speeding cars that jammed on their brakes to avoid a collision. Drivers lowered their windows and let out a fury of curse words. Mathias crept past after the cars came to a stop. Zoe waved a half-hearted apology. As they passed the sign that welcomed them to Umstead State Park, the road turned to gravel and trees swallowed them on both sides.

Russo swerved into the dirt around the first speed bump and pulled over before the second. She rolled down her window and waved towards Mathias. "You got some bootlegger genes in you, Wittles. Nice moving. Now, it's your turn to take the lead, folks."

Zoe nodded and Mathias floored it towards the Visitor's Center. She held her breath and waited to see the cars in the parking lot. As she counted each of them, she exhaled.

Zoe turned and pointed towards one car off to the side. "She's still here."

CHAPTER THIRTY-NINE

CASPER AND DELANEY stood next to her car, which blocked the outlet of the small staff parking lot that shot off of the public lot. The park grounds were quiet and empty, except for a few stragglers who were off on trails and ignorant to the surrounding events. Faces appeared in the office windows. Casper squinted to see who was inside, but to no avail.

Hoagie jumped to Delaney's side and she fed him a treat.

"She didn't say who it was?" Delaney asked.

"Nope. Maybe she was trying to keep things calm here until they can arrive. She said she'd be here in—"

The sound of approaching trucks interrupted their conservation, and they both turned towards the road. Mathias' white Ford F150 barreled down the drive with an unmarked police cruiser close behind. Casper glanced back toward the office and saw that the staff had trickled out of the Visitor's Center and joined them in the parking lot.

Clem stepped out first. Hands on his hips and a smile on his face. Oblivious to the current events and seriousness of the moment. He picked at his teeth with a toothpick and watched

Mathias park the truck sideways in a spot and hop out. Zoe followed with a stone-faced expression that Casper thought resembled regret.

Ernest followed moments later, out of uniform but still wearing his duty belt and his forest green work pants. He glared at Casper and Delaney but hung in the background to watch everything unfold. Despite being left in limbo after his involvement in the case was revealed, Ernest had insisted on lending a hand in the office while Zoe and Mathias stepped away. An obvious last-ditch effort to save face.

Joanne arrived last. Her bright red hair bobbed in the air with each step that she took. A wide-eyed smile was plastered across her face like she'd just gotten a raise. Her smile dissolved as she saw Detective Russo step out of the car behind Zoe and Mathias. Panic appeared in her eyes as they darted back and forth between Russo and Mathias. As if realizing she was visible to her co-workers, she then altered her face to reapply her smile.

"What's this all about, y'all?" Clem asked.

"We just need a minute of everybody's time," Mathias insisted.

"Did you figure out who is dragging my name through the mud?" Ernest shouted.

"There wasn't much left to drag, Ernest!" Clem bellowed and keeled over in laughter.

Zoe nodded towards Detective Russo who stepped toward the group. "We have some updated information about the case that we'd like to discuss with each of you if you have a moment."

Clem nodded. "Take as much as you need. Everything okay?"

"Not exactly, but we'd like to handle these conversations individually."

"Oh gosh, what did you all find out? Did you find the wicked man that did this?" Joanne said in her cartoonish voice.

"Man may not be the correct word," Zoe said and glared at her.

"Ah, goddammit, are you all here trying to pin this on Bigfoot again? Maybe this time it was aliens? Maybe the Loch Ness monster came over from Scotland to screw with the park," Clem shouted. Hoagie growled at him and he stepped back.

"Clem, enough. This isn't a laughing matter," Mathias said. "We'll all be cooperating with Detective Russo to get this case wrapped up."

As Zoe moved forward toward her coworkers, Casper watched Joanne take a half-step backward. He nodded towards her, but Zoe missed the sign. Delaney inched closer to him, gripping Hoagie's leash tight. Her eyes remained fixed on Zoe and Mathias, still trying to piece together the situation at hand.

"Let's just take this one step at a time, okay? We'll speak with each of you individually," Zoe said. "Joanne, maybe we start with you?"

Joanne blushed. "Me? No, I think you'd want to start with somebody important. Maybe Clem here?" As she spoke, she stepped towards Clem and put a playful hand on his shoulder. He laughed and leaned into her.

"Always a kiss-ass, Joanne. But I don't mind hearing it. It's just dill on my pickle," Clem said, beaming.

"No, I just think you're the easiest to manipulate," Joanne spoke with a deeper tone that was unfamiliar to the crowd. Something wiped away and replaced her playful demeanor with a new swagger. As she leaned into Clem, she reached around his side, unbuckled the clip, and grabbed his pistol out of his holster.

Casper pulled Delaney back. Zoe drew her weapon and held it out with a steady arm pointed at Joanne. "Don't do this, Joanne."

Joanne surveyed the crowd. She had three guns pointed in her direction. She made a cautious step to her right. Then another. Casper froze, torn between protecting Delaney, Hoagie, and the others. Joanne stepped closer to him. Then, in one swift movement, she grabbed Casper with one hand and pointed the gun at his head with the other. Then she whispered. "Sorry, but you're one of the few without a gun."

Delaney cried out but was drowned out by Hoagie's barking.

Casper stared into Joanne's eyes but only saw fear. The muffled footsteps of the surrounding park rangers drew Joanne's attention. She pushed the gun into Casper's temple. "Nobody moves another muscle. I don't want to do this, but if you leave me no choice…"

Raindrops plopped down from the sky, one after another. The ominous clouds overhead signaled an oncoming break in the humidity. The air smelled of rain on concrete. He took in the smell as the pistol jammed against his head.

A hiker emerged from the stretch of trail behind the Visitor's Center and drew everybody's attention. As he struggled to comprehend the standoff in the parking lot, he froze. The rangers turned to pass on instructions to the lost soul, and Joanne seized the moment. She kicked Casper in the leg and yelled. "MOVE!"

With Clem's gun pointed back at the others, Joanne shuffled with Casper into the woods and onto the trail. Within moments, the forest had swallowed them whole and none of Casper's rescuers were in sight. His heart rate tripled, then quadrupled. His feet grew clumsy as he tripped over rocks and roots in the trail. He braced himself from the ground with his hands and Joanne kicked at him again. "FASTER!"

Casper wished he'd remembered the trail map enough to know where they were heading. To understand what Joanne's escape plan was, if there even was one. She pushed him up the incline between glances back at the trail behind them. He tried to form words to talk his way towards freedom, but Joanne refused to hear anything besides the sound of hurried steps up the hill and out of harm's way.

At the crest of the hill, Joanne stopped and surveyed her surroundings. Loblolly pines crowded the surrounding land on both sides of the trail. An overgrown laurel obstructed their view to the west. Casper gasped for air. His lungs screamed from the short adrenaline-fueled sprint up the hill. Joanne's head shot back and forth between both sides of the trail, unable to decide which way held freedom and which way held certain punishment or death.

As the seconds ticked by, Casper took in his surroundings. Branches swayed in the strong winds and signaled an oncoming storm. Birds took refuge. Squirrels hopped away and out of sight. The frantic sound of the approaching team grew louder and louder. Joanne remained frozen. A raindrop fell on the tip of Casper's nose. He looked up toward the sky. *Well, at least this is a beautiful place to die.*

CHAPTER FORTY

THE HUMIDITY TURNED, and the sky broke into a downpour. Delaney couldn't see her feet as they pushed through wet leaves and debris as she climbed over the back of the hill. She tied Hoagie's leash around a tree and apologized before rushing towards the others. Zoe and Mathias flanked from the front side, while Ernest and Clem came from the left. They had Joanne surrounded. Delaney pushed out the dark thoughts of what could happen to Casper. She willed him to survive.

At the crest of the hill, Delaney slowed to a strafe. Careful steps. One by one. In the distance, Joanne's red hair flashed like an ember in a forest fire. Through the woods, Clem appeared towards the far side. Ernest was on his heels. Delaney stood still until the booming voice of her cousin echoed through the surrounding pines, accompanied only by the distant barks of Hoagie.

"Joanne, you're surrounded. Put down the weapon."

"No thank you, ma'am," Joanne said and then cackled. "Even in my darkest moments, I can't go out with bad manners."

"Nobody is going anywhere. Just put down the—"

"Don't make me say it again. I'm not putting this down. Somebody is leaving these woods in a body bag. Come hell or high water."

"Joanne, if you kill Casper, the only place you're going is straight to hell or prison. Neither option sounds great, does it?"

"You think I don't know that?" Joanne screamed.

"Just quit the bullshit already!" Ernest shouted from his position.

"You misogynist pig. You should be the first to go!"

Joanne turned the gun towards Ernest and pulled the trigger. Nothing happened. Her face turned pale as she looked at the sleek metal pistol, dumbfounded. Casper threw back an elbow into her stomach and dove off to his right. Joanne stood and waved the gun around at the rangers as they approached. Everybody froze.

"Stay back. I will fire this thing at each of you without a moment of hesitation. I just didn't have a second to check the safety before. I'm still new to this life of crime, after all."

"Joanne, talk to us," Zoe pleaded. "We can help you. We—"

"Talk to you? No, it's too late for that. I've gone too far down this rabbit hole. It started small. I just found an opportunity, and I took it. Everything was going smoothly. Handoffs in the parking lot. The deals were small. Nobody was getting hurt."

Joanne wiped raindrops from her brow. "Then you expert detectives caught on. Suspicion mounted. I heard you all back there discussing how you wanted to bring in drug dogs and make this place like a goddamned border crossing. So, I had to think fast. Luckily, Gil wouldn't shut up about his podcast."

"I don't see how Gil—"

"No, you wouldn't see. You're just a bunch of Yogi Bears out here trying to protect the trees while I would have been a true law enforcement officer making sure that nothing criminal happened in Umstead. But nobody would give me the goddamned chance."

"Joanne, if this is about your application, we can—"

She waved the pistol at Mathias. "No! We can't do anything about that now."

Mathias gritted his teeth. "Then what do you want, Joanne?"

"Your respect would be a great start. I had you all outsmarted for so long. You always underestimated me, but I am cunning. I am sly. Sly like a fox."

"Look, nobody needs to get hurt—" Casper said.

"Hurt? No, that wasn't part of the plan. I helped set up the charade with the Bigfoot costume because I knew you idiots would give it all of your attention."

"But drugs, Joanne?" Zoe asked. "I thought better of you."

"It all fell into place too nicely. Ernest was an easy mark."

Ernest braced both of his hands on his gun and glared at her.

"Ernest was drooling at the mouth when he saw the opportunity to earn a little extra cash to retire with. Little did he know that he was just a patsy. A cog in the machine that we'd built. The empire. And he almost took the fall for it too. But you, Zoe. You had to keep pushing."

"No, I did my job. And your operation fell apart at the seams the second that you laid hands on Wade Buchanon."

Casper's arms were dotted with goosebumps. Joanne laughed. "Wrong place, wrong time. That poor man had no clue what hit him. I regret that somebody got hurt on account of what I was doing. That was never part of the plan."

"But you didn't realize that you got caught. Somebody saw you."

"People think they see things all the time. Like all those hikers who came in and said they saw Bigfoot. Did you believe them like you're believing your eyewitness? No. I doubt that. You hear what you want to hear. Believe things when they fit your narrative. But maybe there's a bigger narrative."

"Joanne. You were wrong. And what you're doing right now is wrong too. Nobody here did anything to harm you. Nobody here meant you any ill will. You were my favorite coworker. I looked forward to each time we had together. I can't believe—"

"I'm sorry, Zoe. But forgive me. You're about to see a whole lot of desk duty."

Joanne pulled the gun and shook it at the surrounding staff. "I did what I had to. Now I'll have to live with the fallout." She stopped speaking and broke into an unhinged fit of laughter. She raised the pistol in front of her. Casper braced himself for impact.

Then, a gunshot rang out through the forest.

The sound boomed and echoed through the trees. Joanne fell onto her back. She wailed in agony and grabbed at her knee.

Smoke trailed out of Zoe's gun as she stood stock-still. Mathias dashed towards Joanne. She fought him at first, but gave in. The pain overtook her. He put pressure on her wound while Zoe secured handcuffs around Joanne's wrists. The rangers propped her up like an injured hiker and escorted her down the trail towards the Visitor's Center. A trail of blood meandered down the pathway as Casper, Delaney and the others followed.

Zoe glanced back at the crimson staining the soil of the trail. The rain washed it away. By morning tomorrow, there would be no sign of blood on any trail. No evidence of the mayhem that brought the entire park staff into the woods. No reason to fear the forest any longer.

Zoe paused for a moment alone in the woods. The case had almost taken everything from her. It drove a wedge between her and Gil. It put Delaney and Casper in harm's way. It layered on a film of grime that Umstead might never wear off, no matter the time or reasoning behind everything.

Delaney stepped up the hill and joined Zoe. "Hell of a shot, Zo."

Zoe grinned. "Remember that Christmas our families spent at the lodge in Virginia? I was maybe ten. Our parents were sick of us, jammed inside because the rain didn't let up. Then Christmas morning came."

"The slingshots."

"The slingshots. We laid on that porch in our best sniper stance and shot everything in the distance. Nothing was off-limits."

"If I recall correctly, you were the one that hit the light bulb to the streetlight."

Zoe laughed. "You've kept that secret long enough. Maybe it's time we come clean to our parents about that one. I bet we won't get grounded for too long."

"So, what made you think of all that now?"

"Simple. I saw you pull your weapon when Joanne was losing it."

"I was prepared to take a shot if the moment came," Delaney said with a half-smile.

"Well, I took it instead. Because just like back then, I'm the better shot."

Delaney grinned. "That you are, Zo."

"I'm not sure Umstead will ever be the same."

"The forest has no memory. Trees don't even pay us any attention at all. The people may be fewer, but that just means more space for you and Gil. And maybe some little ones down the road."

Zoe sighed and tapped the trunk of a red oak. "I'm sorry to you too, Laney."

"Why's that?"

"You came down here for a vacation and I brought you into this case. One involving Bigfoot, a fox, and a disgruntled underpaid employee no less."

Delaney laughed. "The way I see it, you just gave Casper more fodder for his next book. Come on, let's get you home."

They stepped away from the clearing. The pool of blood had disappeared, wiped from the earth by the elements around it. Before long, there was no sign of a struggle at all. Just the distant memory of an incident that few understood or appreciated.

CHAPTER FORTY-ONE

ZOE CREPT into the kitchen with her duty belt in one hand, fingers holding tight to the buttons as to not make a single sound. She eased it onto the table like she was laying a baby in its crib. She had no interest in hearing Gil or anybody else argue about the recommended time off that Mathias had urged her to take after Joanne's arrest.

As she turned to fill the coffeepot, she saw the indicator light was on and the pot was full. She held it close and was surprised to find that it was hot. A fresh batch. A whisper startled her so much she almost dropped the entire pot on the ground.

"Thought you may get a jump on things this morning," Delaney said from her perch in the corner of the kitchen. "It's almost like we're related."

Zoe dove into Delaney's arms so fast that she caused Delaney to spill some of the mug of fresh coffee in her hands.

"HOW'D YOU KNOW?"

Zoe chuckled. "I meant how did you know I'd be up early trying to sneak off."

"Sneak off? I thought you were just trying to beat Gil to the coffeemaker."

Zoe let out a belly laugh and held Delaney tighter.

Delaney broke the embrace and looked at her cousin. "Like I said, we're cut from the same cloth. When we had that mess in Brewster with the Punkhorns, I was back at work as soon as I could get inside the station. It's a hell of a drug. But everybody's got to cope in their own way. People will tell you it's unhealthy, but you just turn the other cheek. You're stubborn. Embrace that."

"And you and Casper?"

"He's packing up as we speak. I told him that if we don't get on the road before sunrise, he'll have to listen to the rest of Gil's podcast."

Zoe snorted, and coffee almost shot out of her nose. "It's not that bad. Plus, he may interview you for season two!"

Delaney rolled her eyes. "I love Gil. He's good for you, despite recent events. But I'll be one happy camper if I do not have to hear about Bigfoot for the next decade."

"Well, last night before bed, Gil mentioned he had a new interest that he wanted to explore. The history of prohibition in North Carolina."

"The man is nothing short of a marathon runner with these research topics. But he's a keeper, Zo."

Casper followed a bounding Hoagie into the room with both of his hands holding their duffel bags. "Did we wake you?"

"She was trying to sneak out before us, Casper. The audacity!" Delaney smirked.

Casper hugged Zoe. "Can I say one last thing about the case before we go?"

She nodded. "What's on your mind?"

"Remember how I kept saying that I thought it was all a setup? Like the Ernest bit was too convenient?"

"And you were correct. Are you just trying to brag now?"

He shook his head. "No. But Joanne said something that's been eating at me. She said that Ernest was "A cog in the machine that we had built"."

"So? I'm not following."

"She said we. Like there was somebody else."

Zoe paused. "I admit I didn't catch that. I'll mull it over and see what Detective Russo thinks about all that. But for now, you're officially off the case."

Casper hugged her again. "We're grateful for your hospitality here. Truly. And for letting us try and help with the case, I—"

"Try and help? Casper, you were an essential piece. Let me know where Mathias and I can send our five-star review."

"You're generous. I—"

"Casper, I'll see you soon. You need to bring my best friend Hoagie back so I can get more cuddles."

Hoagie's tail wagged so hard the entire back half of his body wiggled. Zoe looked up with a smile. "Plus, y'all have to drive back up this way on your way back from Florida, anyway."

"Well, we used up most of our vacation days on the case here, so we're heading back to the Cape. A dreary winter seascape awaits us."

"Aw, I'm sorry that we interrupted your chance to see your parents!"

"This was far more interesting than watching Seinfeld reruns and eating leftovers. It's no bother at all. Thanks for the adventure, Zo. Next time, you and Gil should head up to the Cape."

"You can count on that, Laney."

Zoe leaned back in the creaky wooden chair and propped her feet up on the desk. The air ducts blasted out warm air for the first time in the season, and Zoe basked in the comfort it provided. The clatter of the front entrance to the Visitor's Center woke her from her blissful state. Detective Russo stood over her, grinning ear to ear.

"Well, don't you look comfortable. They still sticking you out at the front desk?"

Zoe smiled. "Just for the day. Grumpy old Mathias told me to take a sick day, but I couldn't stay away. Plus, Mathias has promised me a future full of trails and nature. I'd wager he'll follow through considering Ernest's decision to retire next week."

"I heard about that. Seems fitting."

"How's Joanne?"

"She's in custody. The fox outfit we found hidden beneath the baseboard of her closet matches the fur fibers found in Wade Buchanon's wounds. That may be enough to secure a conviction, despite her claims of innocence."

"She says she's innocent?"

"Of the assault, yes. Says we have it all wrong but won't say more than that. Still, between the eyewitness account of Kyle Pittman and the paper trail left in her apartment, we've got enough to put her away for a long time. That is if we can locate Pittman in time for a trial. He seems to have left town."

"Seems like enough of a case. That's good to hear."

"Joanne was quick to provide a slew of incriminating evidence against her small team of foot soldiers. We have a certain Andy Tucker and Jessica Arwood in custody too. It appears they were her runners. Distributors of a sort."

"Any link between them and her?"

Russo shook her head. "Right now, all we know is that they were both teachers at Pine Hills High. But we'll keep digging."

"Maybe that's what she meant then."

"Beg your pardon? You're not growing shy on me, are you, Zoe?"

Zoe smiled. "Never. But Casper said something about Joanne using a "we" instead of an "I" statement. Like she was part of a team."

"Well, that checks out. I'm still not certain that Joanne Mitchell is smart enough to cook up such a plan on her own."

"Maybe. It doesn't sit right with me though."

"Nobody wants to hear that teachers are so underpaid that they resort to crime. Let alone inside your park. So, I don't blame you."

Zoe sighed. "I'll admit that I'm still grappling with a lot of this. I feel like I should have heard her cries for help. Did she share anything about *why* she did it?"

"Nothing that will help you sleep at night. Just the usual bull-shit. Felt like management overlooked her for the job. She had crippling credit card debt that she'd hidden for years. We're still piecing together how she got involved in the drug trade, but unless she rolls on a distributor, I don't see leniency in her future. Espe-cially if they put Wade Buchanon on the stand. Although he has little memory of the incident."

"So, he's going to make it?"

"Looks that way. He's been released from the hospital, but they're monitoring him for any signs of long-term injuries. All things considered, the doctors think he'll be up and moving around in a few weeks. Could run in next year's marathon if he plays his cards right. His family is over the moon, as you can imagine."

"That's a relief. I was happy to wrap up the case, but he still felt like the victim in all of this. Regardless of how much self-pity I've thrust upon myself."

"This wasn't personal. Joanne continually mentioned you as an ally throughout her statement. If I didn't know you as well as I do, I'd be looking into your financials for anything funky."

Zoe laughed. "You'd find some funky purchases. Considering my fiancé is a Bigfoot enthusiast and I have an obsession with those dark chocolate peanut butter cups from Trader Joe's. But nothing beyond a Park Ranger's measly salary."

Russo smiled. "How is Gil anyway?"

"He's hanging in there. The plan for his book has changed

slightly, but he seems rejuvenated. Last night, we even discussed a date for our wedding. All in all, he's a goofball. But soon, he'll be my husband, the goofball."

Russo nodded. "That's wonderful, Zoe. Well, I have no plans to investigate you further. We've got enough to put some serious leverage on Joanne. Although, I have to admit that I admire some of the complexity of the plan."

"Joanne Mitchell was always clever. But she overstepped."

"You can say that again. But we'll track down whoever is behind this in due time. Anyway, just wanted to wrap things up here. Is Mathias in the back? We've got some paperwork for him to look over."

Zoe nodded and let Russo into the back office. "Thanks, Detective."

"Zoe, thank you. Keep fighting the good fight. Hope next time I see you it is on better terms."

Russo disappeared into the back hallway. Mathias's door slammed shut.

A trickle of cars filled the parking lot. Normalcy resuming. Visitors stepped out in their best autumn attire, ready to take on the balmy temperatures and watch the leaves change before they fall. Zoe glanced out the window and watched a squirrel hopping around in a grass field. She admired the creature's consistency. In a world full of surprises, it was nice to find routine in nature. The birds chirped their usual songs, and the crunch of hiker's boots on the pine needles atop the trail was a pleasant reminder of days past.

CHAPTER FORTY-TWO

A NORTHERN CARDINAL fluttered its wings and came to rest atop the hood of Delaney's car as Casper put the last bag in the trunk and slammed it shut. The noise disturbed the peaceful bird, and it darted away and into the surrounding woods. The dot of red disappeared into the sea of green and brown hues that Casper knew from his short time at Umstead State Park.

Delaney hopped out of the front door and stretched next to the driver's side. "You ready?"

"As I'll ever be," Casper said.

"Hoag?"

He dove between the two front seats and gave each of them a lick on the face. Casper laughed. "I'll take that as a yes."

The traumatic events from the night before had weighed on Casper at first, but like an early morning cold snap, things improved. A full night's sleep had done wonders, but Delaney's support and comfort were the true catalysts. There was also some peace in knowing that justice prevailed. Joanne was off awaiting her charges. Ernest was stepping away from the ranger service. All was right in the world.

The narrow driveway led out to the paved exit road which was crowded by pines and shrubs on their entry to the park but now served as a fitting representation of the sprawling acres that made up the park. Casper's only regret was that he didn't get to see more of what made Umstead such a special place. Still, he understood.

A pack of hikers crossed where the trail bisected the road, and Delaney slowed to a halt. For an early weekday morning, there were a significant number of people out enjoying the warm temperatures that followed the previous night's rainstorm. Skinny legs stuck out of shorts. Hiking poles pressed into the soil, keeping them upright and steady. Dogs zigzagged across the trail, following their noses as they took in the many smells the rain had left behind in the pine needle beds and soil beneath their owner's feet.

The hikers cleared off and faded into the distance. Delaney put her hand on top of Casper's and smiled. "I hope your near-death experience as a hostage didn't sour your impressions of the park."

"I feel like it should have, but somehow it didn't. Zoe's reverence for this place is irresistible. It's contagious. Despite our brief stay, I somehow feel like this place will always hold a special place in our hearts," he said.

"Our hearts? Now you're telling me how to feel? Bold move, Casper Kelly."

"Glad to see that watching me get taken hostage didn't hurt your sarcastic tendencies."

"Nothing could touch that. Don't worry," she said and kissed him on the cheek. "Northbound we go!"

They passed a handful of cars entering through the gate and then turned onto the highway. Just like that, the magic and allure of Umstead dissolved and fast-moving automobiles, exit signs, and ugly concrete medians replaced the trees. "Amazing that little haven sits in the middle of all of this," Casper said, pointing to the surroundings.

"A refuge in more ways than one. Thanks again for coming

with me. Even if we didn't make it down to Florida, this was a perfect vacation for me."

Casper grabbed a notebook and started scribbling. "What in the world are you writing? You're supposed to be keeping me company!" Delaney barked.

"I needed to make sure I didn't forget."

"Forget what?"

"That your ideal vacation involves a crime scene, Bigfoot and criminal masterminds pretending to be low-level administrative employees."

"When you put it that way, sounds like a dream," she laughed. "Did all of this give you any motivation to get back to writing your account of your experiences as a PI?"

"A bit. Although, this one is a bit more absurd than the last. Some may find it hard to believe."

"I think you'd be surprised with people's ability to enjoy the absurd. Plus, you can narrate your very own Bigfoot encounter."

"I realized that Gil never asked you," Casper said.

"Asked me?"

"If you believed. He cornered me on the first chance he got, but somehow you escaped his interrogations."

"By design, I'd imagine."

"Why's that?"

"Because he knows I'm going to tell him what he wants to hear and then tease him behind his back. It's what families do."

"Maybe it's for the best that we didn't make it down to Florida," Casper laughed.

"In due time. But for now, I think we should all steer clear of Bigfoot news for the next while."

"Until Gil's book comes out, you mean."

"Yes, that. But in the meantime, I can't wait to get back to work," Delaney said.

"Same here. Maybe I'll find a few cases that aren't as dire as this one was, but a little more serious than stalking old Sadie Hawkins dates for the Meals on Wheels crowd."

Delaney broke into a fit of raucous laughter.

"What in the world are you giggling about?"

Delaney wiped a tear from her eye and laughed again. "I just can't wait to hear you recount your harrowing tale involving Bigfoot and drug smugglers to the old ladies' book club back in Brewster. They're going to think you've lost it."

"When you put it like that, it does sound a lot like a hallucination."

The radio took over the conversation for a while as NPR shared updates on a recent drug ring that was broken up in Raleigh. There was no mention of The Fox or Umstead State Park, but the story still made both of them smile.

Casper fiddled with the radio and stopped on a familiar tune. Delaney grinned.

"Fitting to leave town with some CCR. Maybe Zoe requested it," she laughed.

The rhythmic guitar jumped in to follow the kick drum. The howling lyrics began and soon they were both singing along to *Fortunate Son*.

As the moment passed, Casper couldn't help but smile. Unlike the man in the song, they were fortunate ones. They were leaving a peaceful wake behind them and marching onward. One foot in front of the other. Bigfoot or small, it didn't matter. One foot in the front of the other. Toward the next adventure.

TWELVE HOURS LATER, Casper lugged his suitcase out of the trunk of Delaney's car and kissed her goodbye. There had been no mention of Raven Rock or any reference to her past life in Boston. Just blissful playlists and crisp fall air through the vents. That was okay. Casper decided that patience was his best friend. He was just happy to have another moment with Delaney in his life.

Hoagie ran up the creaky stairs to the apartment with Casper close behind. Hoagie whined at the door, his tail wagging with anticipation. As Casper slid open the front door, he saw a manila envelope sitting on the floor. Hoagie rushed inside while Casper flipped it over and read the message on the front.

'Everything you need to know about Raven Rock is inside.'

EPILOGUE

THE BEACH WAS PRISTINE. Brochure photo ready and then some. Waves rippled in the distance, careening down from great heights to simmer on the shoreline. The tide crept in and out. Saltwater kissed the toes of the beachgoers. Expertly constructed sand castles washed away with the incoming tide. Kyle Pittman paid no mind to any of that.

He remained focused on the drink in his hand and the stack of books he'd lugged onto the shore with him. He'd made a dent in the library, but nothing like he'd imagined when he arrived two months ago. For the first time in his life, there was no rush. Nowhere to be. No worries.

The sun punished his shoulders. The deep-ruby-red of his skin drew an occasional odd stare from the locals, but few paid it much mind. He pulled the floral print button-down over his arms but let the front hang open. Unbuttoned. Free to blow in the wind.

The ice cubes melted into the mango and orange-infused drink. The color reminded him of a fox. That fiery fur. The distant blaze. A memory of a soon-to-be forgotten past. Here, he wasn't an English teacher struggling to live a comfortable life. He wasn't a former drug runner, nor a former drug kingpin. He had nothing to do with the downfall of Joanne Mitchell. Hell, he wasn't even Kyle anymore. There was a simplistic beauty in his clean slate.

Every time he heard something that sounded like Joanne's name, his stomach hurt. Her love was undying and at first, so was his. A match of two souls wronged throughout their lives. Underestimated. Undervalued. As time grew on, feelings faded. But he saw how easily he could manipulate her to abuse the power and presence that she had within the park. It became a playground where he made the rules.

The act with Andy and Jessica and the others was a tough task. Each day he nearly broke or caved in. Confessed everything. Explained himself. But they wouldn't have understood. Plus, they needed the money. There was a sick joy in watching the relief wash over their lives as they had enough room to breathe. Kyle was angry at the system. The system that failed these hardworking teachers by overworking and underpaying them. So he'd fought back.

He was halfway towards a midday nap when he snapped himself awake. There was enough sunburn on his skin to prove that a foolish endeavor. He folded up his chair, grabbed his backpack and drink, and booked it up the stairs, over the dunes, and into the condo complex parking lot. His two-bedroom bachelor's pad was bigger than anything he had back in North Carolina. And there was no pressure or concern over rent or a mortgage. Here, he paid cash upon arrival.

Gulls squawked as they soared in the clouds. Sand snuck between his toes and he kicked his flip-flop to knock it loose. He glanced up and noticed somebody near his door. No, not near his door. At his front door. It was a woman. A pantsuit with muted tones that didn't belong beside palm trees and tropical birds. He noticed a glimmer of metal on her side. Handcuffs reflected in the bright sunlight.

He dropped the beach chair and considered his next move. The clatter of the aluminum bottom on the sidewalk drew his visitor's attention. She turned and leaned on the railing. Kyle let out a deep exhale.

"Well, hey there, Kyle," she said. Her grin was wider than the coastline. "Nice to see you again. Thought we lost you for a moment."

A life on the run leads you one of two ways. Either you've built the stamina to endure any marathon that comes your way, like a life of new identities and looking over your shoulder. Or it exhausts you. Drains your muscles and your heart of any hope. Leaves you stuck like cement when the moment comes and the starting gun fires.

Kyle nodded and took one last long look at the ocean. The waves danced along the shore. Families basked in the sun and splashed in the shallows. For a moment, he thought he could see the impression in the sand from his chair. Before long, that too would disappear. He smiled and then made his way towards the stairs. When he arrived, he sighed and put out his hands. He opened his mouth and couldn't help but smile. "Detective."

ACKNOWLEDGMENTS

Above all else, thank you for reading. There is nothing that matches the feeling of hearing about how a story touched somebody, made them laugh or kept them turning pages into the night. I hope you loved the story as much as I loved writing it.

I'm beyond grateful to my family and friends for their relentless support and encouragement. Valerie for always being my biggest fan. Peter for positive feedback and input. Kyle for letting me borrow his name and for countless childhood nicknames. Kelsey for the constant cheers, questions and boosts along the way. Megan for being an incredible sounding board and teammate. Harper for long walks and telling me Hoagie should be the main character. Fox for leaning into the role of the villain, maybe a bit too hard. Nick for ranger expertise, positivity and fruit snacks.

Additionally, an enormous thank you to Lisa Orban and the Indies United Publishing House team for their support, community and encouragement. Thanks for taking a chance on me.

The magicians that turned the bones of this story into the words on this page are nothing short of miracle workers. The keen eyes of Aaron Gallagher and Jennie Rosenblum provided an impeccable editing and proofreading team.

A huge thank you to the brave souls who read through an early draft of this and provided feedback. You hold a big(Foot) place in my heart:

- VALERIE B
- NICK D
- NANCY R
- KYLE B
- RYAN M
- SHREYA V
- MARGARET B
- ANN R
- MARY N
- LISA T
- MEGAN L
- FOX L
- HARPER B

ALSO BY BENJAMIN BRADLEY

Welcome to the Punkhorns (Shepard & Kelly Book 1)

The Stash

ABOUT THE AUTHOR

Benjamin Bradley grew up in Parsippany, New Jersey. He currently resides in Durham, North Carolina where he consults for nonprofits and international development organizations. He credits his love of books and writing to his mother who taught him at a young age to appreciate and enjoy stories. Mysteries, thrillers and biographies are among the genres he most frequently reads.